Faith stared at him, apparently sure she hadn't heard him correctly. He couldn't blame her. As soon as the words were out, he'd decided he was crazy.

"You need *what?*"

"A wife." Stone could hear the impatience in his tone, and he forced himself to take deep, slow breaths. Calming breaths.

She spread her hands in confusion, and her smooth brow wrinkled in bewilderment. "But how can I help you with that? I doubt I know anyone who—"

"Faith." His deep voice stopped her tumbling words. "I'd like *you* to be my wife."

Her eyes widened. Her mouth formed a perfect "O" of surprise. She put a hand up and pointed at herself as if she needed confirmation that she hadn't lost her mind, and her lips soundlessly formed the word "Me?"

He nodded. "Yes. You."

Dear Reader,

Celebrate the rites of spring with six new passionate, powerful and provocative love stories from Silhouette Desire!

Reader favorite Anne Marie Winston's *Billionaire Bachelors: Stone*, our March MAN OF THE MONTH, is a classic marriage-of-convenience story, in which an overpowering attraction threatens a platonic arrangement. And don't miss the third title in Desire's glamorous in-line continuity DYNASTIES: THE CONNELLYS, *The Sheikh Takes a Bride* by Caroline Cross, as sparks fly between a sexy-as-sin sheikh and a feisty princess.

In *Wild About a Texan* by Jan Hudson, the heroine falls for a playboy millionaire with a dark secret. *Her Lone Star Protector* by Peggy Moreland continues the TEXAS CATTLEMAN'S CLUB: THE LAST BACHELOR series, as an unlikely love blossoms between a florist and a jaded private eye.

A night of passion produces major complications for a doctor and the social worker now carrying his child in *Dr. Destiny*, the final title in Kristi Gold's miniseries MARRYING AN M.D. And an ex-marine who discovers he's heir to a royal throne must choose between his kingdom and the woman he loves in Kathryn Jensen's *The Secret Prince*.

Kick back, relax and treat yourself to all six of these sexy new Desire romances!

Enjoy!

Joan Marlow Golan

Joan Marlow Golan
Senior Editor, Silhouette Desire

Please address questions and book requests to:
Silhouette Reader Service
U.S.: 3010 Walden Ave., P.O. Box 1325, Buffalo, NY 14269
Canadian: P.O. Box 609, Fort Erie, Ont. L2A 5X3

Billionaire
Bachelors: Stone
ANNE MARIE WINSTON

Published by Silhouette Books
America's Publisher of Contemporary Romance

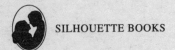 SILHOUETTE BOOKS

ISBN 0-373-76423-5

BILLIONAIRE BACHELORS: STONE

Visit Silhouette at www.eHarlequin.com

Printed in U.S.A.

Books by Anne Marie Winston

Silhouette Desire

Best Kept Secrets #742
Island Baby #770
Chance at a Lifetime #809
Unlikely Eden #827
Carolina on My Mind #845
Substitute Wife #863
Find Her, Keep Her #887
Rancher's Wife #936
Rancher's Baby #1031
Seducing the Proper Miss Miller #1155
*The Baby Consultant #1191
*Dedicated to Deirdre #1197
*The Bride Means Business #1204
Lovers' Reunion #1226
The Pregnant Princess #1268
Seduction, Cowboy Style #1287
Rancher's Proposition #1322
Tall, Dark & Western #1339
A Most Desirable M.D. #1371
Risqué Business #1407
Billionaire Bachelors: Ryan #1413
Billionaire Bachelors: Stone #1423

*Butler County Brides

ANNE MARIE WINSTON

RITA Award finalist and bestselling author Anne Marie Winston loves babies she can give back when they cry, animals in all shapes and sizes and just about anything that blooms. When she's not writing, she's chauffeuring children to various activities, trying *not* to eat chocolate or reading anything she can find. She will dance at the slightest provocation and weeds her gardens when she can't see the sun for the weeds anymore. You can learn more about Anne Marie's novels by visiting her Web site at www.annemariewinston.com.

To all the nurses at the Waynesboro Hospital
who have shared my midnight vigils. My thanks do not
begin to express my appreciation for your kindnesses.

Prologue

"**S**mythe Corp. will be yours...on one condition." Eliza Smythe's eyes narrowed as she studied her only son.

Stone Lachlan stood with one arm negligently braced on the mantel above the marble fireplace in his mother's Park Avenue apartment in New York City. Not even the flicker of an eyelash betrayed any emotion. He wasn't about to let his mother know what her offer meant to him. Not until it was his and she couldn't take it away.

"And what might that condition be?" He lifted the crystal highball glass to his lips and drank, keeping the movement slow and lazy. Disinterested.

"You get married—"

"Married!" Stone nearly choked on the fine Scotch malt whiskey.

"And settle down," his mother added. "I want

grandchildren one of these days while I'm still young enough to enjoy them.''

He set his glass on a nearby marble-topped table with a snap. It took him a moment to push away the hurtful memories of a small boy whose mother had been too busy to bother with him. His mouth twisted cynically. ''If you plan to devote yourself to grandchildren as totally as you did me, why are you planning to retire? It doesn't take much time to give a nanny instructions once a week or so.''

His mother flinched. ''If it's any consolation to you, I regret the way you were raised,'' she said, and he could hear pain in her voice. ''If I had it to do over…''

''If you had it to do over, you'd do exactly the same thing,'' Stone interrupted her. The last thing he needed was to have his mother pretending she cared. ''You'd immerse yourself in your family's company until you'd dragged it back from the brink of bankruptcy. And you'd keep on running it because you were the only one left.''

His mother bowed her head, acknowledging the truth of his words. ''Perhaps.'' Then she squared her shoulders and he could see her shaking off the moment of emotion. Just as she'd shaken him off so many times. ''So what's your decision? Do you accept my offer?''

''I'm thinking,'' he said coolly. ''You drive a hard bargain. Why the wife?''

''It's time for you to think about heirs,'' his mother said. ''You're nearly thirty years old. You'll have responsibilities to both Smythe Corp. and Lachlan International and you should have children to follow in your footsteps.''

God, he wished she was kidding but he doubted his mother had ever seen the point of a joke in her entire life. A wife...? He didn't want to get married. Hadn't ever really been tempted, even. A shrink would have a field day with that sentiment, would probably pronounce him scarred by his childhood. But the truth, as Stone saw it, was simply that he didn't want to have to answer to anyone other than himself.

Where in hell was he going to get a wife, anyway? Oh, finding a woman to marry him would be easy. There were dozens of fresh young debutantes around looking for Mr. Rich and Right. The problem would be finding one he could stand for more than five minutes, one that wouldn't attempt to take him to the cleaners when the marriage ended. When the marriage ended...that was it! He'd make a temporary marriage, pay some willing woman a lump sum for the job of acting as his wife for a few weeks.

"Draw up the papers, Mother." His voice was clipped. "I'll find a wife."

"Which is why it's conditional."

That got his attention. "Conditional? What—you want final approval?" Another thought occurred to him. "Or you're giving me some time limit by which I have to tie the knot?"

Eliza shook her head. "The last thing I want you to do is rush into marriage. I'd rather you wait until you find the right woman. But at least now I know you'll be thinking about it. The condition is that once you marry, the marriage has to last for one year—with both of you living under the same roof—before the company becomes yours."

One year... His agile mind immediately saw the

fine print. He would find a bride, all right. And the minute the ink was dry on the contract with his mother, there would be a quiet annulment. A twinge of guilt pricked at his conscience but he shrugged it off. He didn't owe his mother *anything*. And it would serve her right for thinking she could manipulate his life this way.

He smiled, trying to mask his newfound satisfaction. "All right, Mother. You've got a deal. I find a bride, you give me your dearest possession."

Eliza stood, her motions jerky. "I know I haven't been much of a mother to you, Stone, but I do care. That's why I want you to start looking for a wife. Being single might seem appealing for a while, but it gets awfully lonely."

He shrugged negligently, letting the words hit him and bounce off. No way was he going to let her start tugging at his heartstrings after all this time. She was the one who had chosen to leave. "Whatever."

Eliza started for the door. "At least give it some thought." She sighed. "I never thought I'd say it, but I'm actually looking forward to having some free time."

"I never thought you'd say it, either." And he hadn't. His mother lived and breathed the company that had come to her on her father's death when she was barely twenty-five. She'd loved it far more than she had Stone or his father, as his dad had pointed out.

Smythe Corp. He'd resigned himself to waiting for years to inherit his mother's corporation. But he'd never stopped dreaming. Now he would be able to implement the plans he'd considered for years. He'd merge Smythe Corp. with Lachlan Enterprises, the company that had been his father's until his death eight years ago.

As his mother took her leave, he moved into his office, still thinking about finding the right woman to agree to what sounded like an insane idea. A temporary wife. Why not? Marriage, as far as he could tell, was a temporary institution anyway. One he had never planned to enter. But if marriage was what it took, then marriage was what his mother would get.

While he turned the problem over in his head, he thumbed through the day's mail. His hand slowed as he came to a plain brown envelope. In the envelope was the report he received quarterly, giving him updates on his ward, Faith Harrell.

Faith. She'd been a gawky twelve-year-old the first time he'd seen her. He'd been fresh out of college, and they both were reeling from the death of their two fathers in a boating accident a month earlier. He'd been absolutely stunned, he recalled, when Faith's mother had begged him to become her guardian.

A guardian…him? It sounded like something out of the last century. But he hadn't been able to refuse. Mrs. Harrell had multiple sclerosis. She feared the disease's advance. And worse, she'd been a quietly well-to-do socialite for her entire married life, pursuing genteel volunteer work and keeping her home a charming, comfortable refuge for her husband. She knew nothing of finances and the world of business. They'd been married for a long, long time before they'd had Faith and their world had revolved around her. His father would have wanted him to make sure Randall Harrell's family was taken care of.

And so Faith became his ward. He'd taken care of

her, and of her mother, in a far more tangible way when he'd discovered the dismal state of Randall's investments. The man had been on the brink of ruin. Faith and her mother were practically penniless. And so Stone had quietly directed all their bills to him throughout the following years. He'd seen no reason to distress the fragile widow with her situation, and even less to burden a young girl with it. It was what his father would have done, and it certainly wasn't as if it imposed a financial strain on his own immense resources.

Faith. Her name conjured up an image of a slender schoolgirl in a neat uniform though he knew she hadn't worn uniforms since leaving her boarding school. It had been more than a year since he'd seen her. She'd become a lovely young thing as she'd grown up and she probably was even prettier now. She would be finishing her junior year at college in a few months. And though he hadn't seen her in person recently, he looked forward to reading the update on her from the lawyer who had overseen the monetary disbursements to Faith and her mother.

He slit the envelope absently as he returned to the problem of where to find a temporary wife.

Five minutes later, he was rubbing the back of his neck in frustration as he spoke to the man who provided the updates on Faith Harrell. ''What do you mean, she withdrew from school two weeks ago?''

One

A huge, hard hand clamped firmly about her wrist as Faith Harrell turned from the Carolina Herrerra display she was creating in the women's department of Saks Fifth Avenue.

"What in *hell* are you doing?" a deep, masculine voice growled.

Startled, Faith looked up. A long way up, into the furious face of Stone Lachlan. Her heart leaped, then began to tap-dance in her chest as pleasure rose so swiftly it nearly choked her. She hadn't seen Stone since he'd taken her out for lunch one day last year— he was the last person she had imagined meeting today! Her pulse had begun to race at the sound of his growling tones and she hoped he didn't feel it beneath his strong fingers.

"Hello," she said, smiling. "It's nice to see you, too."

He merely stared at her, one dark eyebrow rising. "I'm waiting for an explanation."

Stone was nearly ten years her senior. His father and hers had been best friends and she'd grown up visiting with Stone and his father occasionally, chasing the big boy who gave her piggyback rides and helped her dance by letting her stand on his feet. He'd been merely a pleasant, distant-relation sort of person until their fathers had died together in a squall off Martha's Vineyard eight years ago. Since then, Stone had been her guardian, making sure her mother's multiple sclerosis wasn't worsened by any sort of stress. Technically she supposed she still was his ward, despite the fact that she'd be twenty-one in November, just eight months away. And despite the additional fact that she was penniless and didn't need a guardian anyway.

Stone. Her stomach fluttered with nervous delight and she silently admonished herself to settle down and behave like an adult. She'd been terribly infatuated with him by the time she was a young teenager.

He'd teased her, told her jokes and tossed her in the air. And she'd been smitten with the fierce pain of unrequited love. Though she'd told herself it was just a crush and she'd outgrown him, her body's involuntary reactions to his nearness now called her a liar. *Ridiculous,* she told herself sternly. *You haven't seen the man in months. You barely know him.*

But Stone had kept tabs on her since their fathers' deaths, though his busy schedule apparently hadn't permitted him to visit often. He'd remembered her at Christmas and on her birthday, and she'd occasionally gotten postcards from wherever he happened to be in the world, quick pleasantries scrawled in a strong masculine hand. It hadn't been much, she supposed, but to a young girl at a quiet boarding school, it had been enough.

And she knew from comments he'd made in his infrequent letters that he had checked on her progress at boarding school and at college, which she'd attended for two and a half years.

Until she'd learned the truth.

The truth. Her pleasure in his appearance faded.

"I work here," she said quietly, gathering her dignity around her. She should be furious with Stone for what he'd done, but she couldn't stop herself from drinking in the sight of his large, dark-haired form, so enormous and out of place among the delicate, feminine clothing displays.

"You quit school," he said, his strong, tanned features dark with displeasure.

"I temporarily stopped taking classes," she corrected. "I hope to return part-time eventually." Then she remembered her shock and humiliation on the day she'd learned that Stone had paid for her education and every other single thing in her life since her father's death. "And in any case, I couldn't have stayed. I needed a job."

Stone went still, his fingers relaxing on her wrist although he didn't release her, and she sensed his sudden wariness. "Why do you say that?"

She shook the index finger of her free hand at him. "You know very well why, so don't pretend innocence." She surveyed him for a moment, unable to prevent the wry smile that tugged at her lips. "You'd never pull it off."

He didn't smile back. "Have lunch with me. I want to talk to you."

She thought for a moment. "About what?"

"Things," he said repressively. His blue eyes were dark and stormy and he took a moment to look at their surroundings. "You can't keep this up."

She smiled at his ill temper. "Of course I can. I'm not a millionaire, it helps to pay the rent." Then she remembered the money. "Actually, I want to talk to you, too."

"Good. Let's go." Stone started to tow her toward the escalator, but Faith stiffened her legs and resisted.

"Stone! I'm working. I can't just leave." She waved a hand toward the rear of the department. "Let me check with my supervisor and see what time I can take my lunch break."

He still held her wrist and she wondered if he could feel her pulse scramble beneath his fingers. He searched her face for a long moment before he nodded once, short and sharp. "All right. Hurry."

Faith turned and walked to the back of the store at a ladylike pace. She refused to let Stone see how much his presence unsettled her. Memories ran through her head in a steady stream.

When he'd come to visit a few months after the funeral to help her mother tell her what they had decided, he'd been grieving, but even set in unsmiling severe lines, his face had been handsome. She'd been drawn even more than ever to his steady strength and charismatic presence. He talked about the friendship their fathers had shared since their days as fraternity brothers in college but she'd known even before he started to talk that he'd feel responsible for her. He was just that kind of man.

He intended to continue to send her to a nearby private school in Massachusetts, he told her, and to make sure that her mother's care was uninterrupted and her days free of worry. And though she hadn't known it at the time, Stone had taken over the burden of those debts. At the time of his death, her father had been nearly insolvent.

"Faith!" One of the other saleswomen whispered at her as she rushed by. "Who is that gorgeous, gorgeous man standing over there? I saw you talking to him."

Faith threaded her way through the salespeople gathering in the aisle. "A family friend," she replied. Then she saw Doro, her manager. "What time will I have my break today?"

Doro's eyes were alive with the same avid curiosity dancing in the other womens' faces. "Does *he* want you to have lunch with him?"

Wordlessly Faith nodded.

"That's Stone Lachlan!" One of the other clerks rushed up, dramatically patting her chest. "Of the steel fortune Lachlans. And his mother is the CEO of Smythe Corp. Do you know how much he's worth?"

"Who cares?" asked another. "He could be penniless and I'd still follow him anywhere. What a total babe!"

"Sh-h-h." Doro hustled the others back to work. Then she turned back to Faith. "Go right now!" The manager all but took her by the shoulders and shoved her back in Stone's direction.

Faith was amused, but she understood Stone's potent appeal. Even if he hadn't been so good-looking, he exuded an aura of power that drew women irresistibly.

Quietly she gathered her purse and her long black

wool coat, still a necessity in New York City in March. Then she walked back to the front of the women's department where Stone waited. He put a hand beneath her elbow as he escorted her from the store and she shivered at the touch of his hard, warm fingers on the tender bare flesh of her neck as he helped her into her coat and gently drew her hair from beneath the collar.

He had a taxi waiting at the curb and after he'd handed her into the car, he took a seat at her side. "The Rainbow Room," he said to the driver.

Faith sat quietly, absorbing as much of the moment as she could. This could very well be the last time she ever shared a meal with him. Indeed, this could be the last time she ever saw him, she realized. He had taken her out to eat from time to time when she was younger and he'd come to visit her at school. She'd never known when he was going to show up and whisk her off for the afternoon—Lord, she'd lived for those visits. But she and Stone lived in different worlds now and it was unlikely their paths would cross.

At the restaurant, they were seated immediately. She sat quietly until Stone had ordered their meals. Then he squared his big shoulders, spearing her with an intense look. "You can't work as a shop girl."

"Why not? Millions of women do and it hasn't seemed to harm them." Faith toyed with her water glass, meeting his gaze. "Besides, I don't have a choice. You know as well as I do that I have no money."

He had the grace to look away. "You'd have been taken care of," he said gruffly.

"I know, and I appreciate that." She folded her

hands in her lap. "But I can't accept your charity. I'd like to know how much I owe you for everything you did in the past eight years—"

"I didn't ask you to pay me back." He leaned forward and she actually found herself shrinking back from the fierce scowl on his face.

"Nonetheless," she said as firmly as she could manage, given the way her stomach was quivering, "I intend to. It will take me some time, but if we draw up a schedule—"

"No."

"I beg your pardon?"

"I said no, you may not pay me back." His voice rose. "Dammit, Faith, your father would have done the same if I'd been in your shoes. I promised your mother I'd take care of you. She trusts me. Besides, it's an honor thing. I'm only doing what I know my father would have done."

"Ah, but your father didn't make risky investments that destroyed his fortune," she said, unable to prevent a hot wash of humiliation from warming her cheeks.

"He could have." Stone's chin jutted forward in a movement she recognized from the time he'd descended on the school to talk to her math teacher about giving her a failing grade on a test she'd been unable to take because she'd had pneumonia. "Besides," he said, "it's not as if it's made a big dent in my pocketbook. Last time I checked, there were a few million left."

She shook her head. "I still don't feel right about taking your money. Do you have any idea how I felt when I learned that you'd been paying my way for years?"

"How did you find out, anyway?" He ignored her question.

"In February I went to the bank to talk about my father's investments—I thought it would be good for me to start getting a handle on them since you'd no longer be responsible for me after my twenty-first birthday, which is coming up later this year. I assumed I'd take on responsibility for my mother's finances then, as well. That's when I learned that every item in my family's budget for *eight years* had been paid for by you." Despite her vow to remain calm, tears welled in her eyes. "I was appalled. Someone should have told me."

"And what good would that have done, other than to distress you needlessly?"

"I could have gotten a job right out of high school, begun to support myself."

"Faith," he said with ill-concealed impatience. "You were not quite thirteen years old when your father died. Do you really think I would have left you and your mother to struggle alone?"

"It wasn't your decision to make," she insisted with stubborn pride, swallowing the tears.

"It was," he said in a tone that brooked no opposition. "It *is*. Your mother appointed me your guardian. Besides, if you finish your education you'll be able to get a heck of a lot better job than working as a salesclerk at Saks."

"Does my mother know the truth?"

Stone shook his head. "She believes I oversee your investments and take care of the bills out of the income. Her doctors tell me stress is bad for MS patients. Why distress her needlessly?"

It made sense. And in an objective way, she admired his compassion. But it still horrified her to think of the money he'd spent.

The waiter returned then with their meal and the conversation paused until he'd set their entrées before them. They both were quiet for the next few moments.

Stone ate with deep concentration, his dark brows drawn together, obviously preoccupied with something.

She hated to be keeping him from something important but when she said as much, he replied, "You were the only thing on my agenda for today."

Really, there wasn't anything she could say in response to *that,* she thought, suppressing a smile. "Since that's the case," she finally said, "I'd really like to have an accounting of how much I owe you—"

"*Do not* ask me that one more time." Stone's deep voice vibrated with suppressed anger.

She gave up. If Stone wouldn't tell her, she could figure out a rough estimate, at least, by combining tuition fees with a living allowance. And she should be able to get a record of her mother's fees from her doctor. "I have to get back to work soon," she said in the coolest, most polite manner she could muster.

Stone's head came up; he eyed her expression. "Hell," he said. "You're already mad at me; I might as well get it all over with at once."

"I'd prefer that you don't swear in my presence." She lifted her chin. Then his words penetrated. "What do you mean?"

"You're not going back to work."

"Excuse me?" Her voice was frosty.

He hesitated. "I phrased that badly. I want you to quit work."

She stared at him. "Are you crazy? And live on what?"

He scowled. "I told you I'd take care of you."

"I can take care of myself. I won't always be a salesclerk. I'm taking night classes starting in the summer," she said. Despite her efforts to remain calm, her voice began to rise. "It's going to take longer this way but I'll finish."

"What are you studying?" His sudden capitulation wasn't expected.

She eyed him with suspicion. "Business administration and computer programming. I'd like to start my own business in Web design one of these days."

His eyebrows rose. "Ambitious."

"And necessary," she said. "Mama's getting worse. She's going to need 'round-the-clock care one of these days. I need to be able to provide the means for her to have it."

"You know I'll always take care of your mother."

"That's not the point!" She wanted to bang her head—or his—against the table in frustration.

"My father would have expected me to take care of you. *That's* the point." He calmly sat back against the banquette, unfazed by her aggravation, an elegant giant with the classic features of a Greek god, and she was struck again by how handsome he was. When they'd entered The Rainbow Room, she'd been aware of the ripple of feminine interest that his presence had attracted. She'd been ridiculously glad that she was wearing her black Donna Karan today. It might be a few years old but it was a gorgeous garment and she felt more confident simply slipping it on. Then she remembered that *his* money had paid for the dress, and her pleasure in her appearance drained away.

"I'm sure your father would be pleased that you've done your duty," she said with a note of asperity. "But we will *not* continue to accept your charity."

He grimaced. "Bullhead."

"Look who's talking." But she couldn't resist the gleam in his eye and she smiled back at him despite the gnawing feeling of humiliation that had been lodged in her belly since the day she'd found out she was essentially a pauper. "Now take me back to work. My lunch hour is almost over."

He heaved an impatient sigh. "This is against my better judgment."

She leaned forward, making her best effort to look intimidating. "Just think about how miserable I will make your life if you don't. I'm sure your judgment will improve quickly."

He shot her a quirky grin. "I'm shaking in my boots."

He didn't want to notice her.

She had been an unofficial little sister during his youth, and his responsibility since her father had died. She was ten years younger than he was. He was her guardian, for God's sake!

But as he handed her back into the car after their meal, his eye was caught by the slim length of her leg in the elegant high heels as she stepped in, by the way her simple dress hugged the taut curve of her thigh as she slid across the seat, by the soft press of pert young breasts against the fabric of the black coat as she reached for her seat belt.

He'd seen her standing in the store long before she had noticed him, her slender figure strikingly displayed in a black dress that, although it was perfectly discreet, clung to her in a way that made a man want to strip it off and slide his hands over the smooth curves beneath. Made *him* want to touch, to pull the pins out of her shining coil of pale hair and watch it slither down over her shoulders and breasts, to set his mouth to the pulse that beat just beneath the delicate skin along her white throat and taste—

Enough! *She's not for you.*

Grimly he dragged his mind back from the direction in which it wanted to stray.

He hated the idea of her wearing herself out hustling in retail for eight hours a day, and he figured he'd give it one more try. The only woman he'd ever known who really enjoyed working was his mother. Faith shouldn't be working herself into exhaustion. She should be gracing someone's home, casting her gentle influence around a man, making his life an easier place to be. He knew it was an archaic attitude and that most modern women would hit him over the head for voicing such a thought. But he'd lived a childhood without two parents because his own mother had put business before family. He *knew*, despite all the Superwoman claims of the feminist movement, that a woman couldn't do it all.

Diplomatically he only said, "Why don't you go back to school for the rest of the semester? Then this summer we can talk about you finding a job."

Her eyes grew dark and her delicate brows snapped together. "You will *not* give me money.

More money," she amended. "I'm not quitting work. I need the money. Besides, it's too late in the semester to reenroll. I've missed too much."

He looked across the car at her, seated decorously with her slender feet placed side by side, her hands folded in her lap and her back straight as a ramrod. Her hair was so fair it nearly had a silver sheen to it where the winter sun struck it, and her eyes were a pure lake-gray above the straight little nose. She had one of the most classically lovely faces he'd ever seen, and she looked far too fragile to be working so hard. The only thing that marred the picture of the perfect lady was the frown she was aiming his way. The contrast was adorable and he caught himself before he blurted out how beautiful she was in a snit.

Then he realized that beautiful or not, she was as intransigent as a mule who thought she was carrying too heavy a load. "All right," he said. "You can keep doing whatever you want. Within reason."

"Your definition of reason and mine could be quite different." Her tone was wry and her frown had relaxed. "Besides, in eight more months, you won't have any authority to tell me what to do. Why don't you start practicing now?"

He took a deep breath, refusing to snarl. He nearly told her that no matter how old she got she'd always be his responsibility, but the last thing he needed was for her to get her back up even more. Then he recalled the image of her stricken face, great gray eyes swimming with the tears she refused to give in to as she told him how she'd found out about her financial affairs, and he gentled his response to a more reasonable request. "Would you at least consider a different kind of job? Something that isn't so demanding?''

She was giving him another distinctly suspicious look. ''Maybe. But I won't quit today.''

He exhaled, a deep, exaggeratedly patient sigh. ''Of course not.''

When the taxi rolled to a stop in front of Saks, he took her elbow as she turned toward the door. ''Wait,'' he said before she could scramble out.

She turned back and looked at him, her gray eyes questioning.

''Have dinner with me tonight.''

Could her eyes get any wider? ''Dinner?''

He knew how she felt. He hadn't planned to ask her; the words had slipped out before he'd thought about them. Good Lord. ''Um, yes,'' he said, wondering if thirty was too early for the onset of senility. ''I'll pick you up. What's your address?''

She lived on the upper West Side, in a small apartment that would have been adequate for two. But he knew from the talk they had shared over lunch that she had at least two roommates from the names she'd mentioned.

''How many people do you live with?'' he asked dubiously, looking around as she unlocked the door and ushered him in.

''Three other girls,'' she answered. ''Two to each bedroom. Two of us work days and two work nights so it's rare that we're all here at the same time.''

Just then, a door opened and a girl in a black leotard and denim overalls came down the hall. Stone examined her with disbelief. She was a redhead, at least mostly. There was a blue streak boldly marching through the red near the left front side of her curly hair. She had a wide, friendly smile and green eyes that were sparkling with interest.

"Well, hey," she said. "Like, I hate to tell you, handsome, but you *so* do not fit in here."

He couldn't keep himself from returning the grin. "My Rolex gave me away?"

"Gretchen, this is Stone Lachlan," Faith said. "Stone, one of my roommates, Gretchen Vandreau."

"Pleased to meet you." Gretchen dropped a mock-curtsy, still beaming.

"You also, Miss Vandreau." He grinned again as her eyes widened.

"Are you—oh, wow, you are! *The* Lachlans." Her eyebrows shot up as she eyed Faith. "Where did you find him?"

"Actually I found her," Stone said. "Faith and I are old friends." He turned to Faith. "Are you ready?"

"Ready? Like, to go out?" Gretchen looked from one to the other with delight. "You go, girlfriend."

"It's not like *that,*" she said to Gretchen.

"Depends on what *that* is," Stone inserted.

Faith turned and glared at him. "Stone—"

"Better hurry, I have reservations for eight." He felt an odd sense of panic as he gauged the mulish expression on her face. Was she having second thoughts? Was she going to back out? He had to battle the urge to simply pick her up and carry her back down to the car.

She retrieved a black cape from the small coat closet with her friend chattering along behind her. He stepped in to help her on with the garment, and they went out the door to the sound of Gretchen's enthusiastic, "Have a blast!"

He took her elbow and urged her into the elevator, conscious of a ridiculous sense of relief sweeping through him as they exited the cramped apartment. It was only that he felt it was his duty to take care of her, he assured himself. Faith didn't belong in a crowded apartment or behind a counter in a department store. Her family had intended that she be gently raised, probably with the idea that she'd marry a polite young man of the upper class one day and raise polite, well-mannered upper-class children. After all, she'd been sent to the best private schools, had learned the sometimes ridiculous rules that accompanied moving in society.

He wished the idea didn't fill him with such a sense of…unease. That was all it was. He wanted the best for her and it would be up to him to be sure any suitors were suitable.

He surveyed her covertly as they stood in the elevator, waiting for the ground floor. Her blond hair was smoothly swept back into a shining knot at the back of her head and the harsh lighting in the elevator made it gleam with silvery highlights. She was chewing on her bottom lip; he reached out and touched it with his index finger to get her to stop. Alarm bells went off in his head as a strange jolt of electric awareness shot through his body.

He stared down at her. She had her gaze fixed on the floor and he had to restrain himself from reaching for her chin and covering her lips with his own. What would she taste like?

Then he realized what he was thinking…totally

inappropriate thought to be having about a girl who was like his little sister. Again.

Little sister? Since when do you wonder how your little sister's curves would feel pressed up against you?

He almost growled aloud to banish his unruly thoughts and Faith's gray eyes flashed to his face with a wary look he thought was probably normally aimed at large predators.

"Something wrong?" he asked.

"No." Then she shook her head. "That's not true. Why are you doing this?"

He gazed calmly back at her. "Dinner, you mean?"

She nodded.

"I'm your guardian. It struck me today that I haven't done a very good job of it, either, so I thought we'd spend a little more time together. You can tell me more about your plans."

She nodded again, as if his explanation made sense.

The ride to the small, quiet Italian restaurant where he'd made reservations was a short one. As the maître d' showed them to their table, Faith caught his eye. As the man walked away, she whispered, "If this isn't a Mafia haven, I don't know what is!"

He chuckled, surprised she'd picked up on it. He'd been coming here for years—the food was reputed to be some of the best Northern Italian cuisine in the city. But the waiters, the bartender, certainly the man who appeared to be the owner greeting guests, had an air of authority, underlaid with an indefinable air of menace. "It's probably the safest place to be in Manhattan," he said.

Over dinner, he asked her questions about her interest in computers.

"I had a knack for it," she told him, "and I started helping out in the computer lab at school. It got so that the instructors were coming to me with questions about how to do things, and how to fix things they'd messed up. That led me into programming and eventually I set up the school's Web site. And once I did that, other people began to ask me to design their sites. It occurred to me that I could make a living doing something I really enjoy, so I decided on a double major in computers and business."

"You're planning to open your own company when you get your degree?"

She nodded, and her eyes shone with enthusiasm. "Eventually. I think I'd like the challenge. But I'll probably start at an established firm." She paused and her gaze grew speculative. "You had to take over Lachlan after your father passed away, and you've clearly been successful at it. You can give me some pointers."

He shrugged. Discussing business with Faith was hardly at the top of his list of things he wanted to do. "I'm sure you'll have no trouble."

Their dinners arrived and while they ate, he inquired about her mother's health.

"She isn't able to get around without using a motorized scooter now," she said, her face sobering. "She's sixty, and the disease has started to accelerate. Recently she's been having a lot of trouble with her vision. Some days are better than others. But it's only a matter of time before she needs live-in assistance or she has to go to some kind of assisted care facility. She wasn't happy that I'm working, either, but we're going to be facing some serious expenses one of these days." He could hear the frustration in her voice.

"She's only thinking of you," he said. "She wants you to have the freedom and enjoy normal experiences for a young woman your age."

Moments later, Faith excused herself from the table and made her way to the ladies' room. As he watched her walk across the room, he was struck again by her elegance and poise. Every man in the room watched her and he caught himself frowning at a few of them in warning.

That was ridiculous. He wasn't her keeper.

Well, in fact he supposed he was. But this wasn't the Dark Ages and she didn't need his permission to accept a suitor. Or a husband, for that matter.

He didn't like that thought. Not at all. Faith was still very young, and she fairly screamed, "Innocent." She could easily be taken advantage of now that she wasn't in the somewhat protected environment of an all-girls' college. She was still his ward, though in her mind, at least, it was a mere technicality. In his, it was altogether different. He was supposed to take care of her. And he'd never forgive himself if she came to harm, even if it was only getting her heart broken by some cad. It frustrated the hell out of him that he wasn't going to be able to keep her safe.

Then the perfect solution to his frustration popped into his head. He could marry her!

Marry her? Was he insane? They were ten years apart in age, far more than that in experience. But, he decided, the kind of experience he was thinking of could play no part in a marriage with Faith. It would be strictly a platonic arrangement, he assured himself. Simply an arrangement that would help him achieve a goal and protect her at the same time. If she was married, Faith wouldn't be a target for trouble. In another year or so she'd be more worldly, and the best part was that he would be able to keep her safe during that time.

He was going to have to marry to satisfy his mother's conditions anyway. And if they married soon, as soon as possible, then he'd be only a year away from achieving the goal of which he'd dreamed for years. He would be able to merge Smythe Corp. and Lachlan Industries into one bigger and better entity.

Then he forgot about business as Faith appeared again. She walked toward him as if he'd called to her, and as she drew closer he could see her smiling at him. He smiled back, knowing that the other men in the place had to be envying him. Long and lean, she had a smooth, easy walk with a regal carriage that ensured instant attention when paired with that angelic face. He doubted she even realized it.

As she passed one of the waiters, the man flashed a white smile at her. She gave him a warm smile in return, and she had no idea that he'd turned to watch her back view as she continued on through the restaurant to their table.

And *that* was exactly why she needed his protection, Stone thought grimly. He stood as she arrived and walked around to settle her in her chair. She glanced up at him over her shoulder with the same sweet smile she'd just given the waiter, and he felt his gut clench in response. She was far too potent for her own good.

"So," he said, picking up his water and taking a healthy gulp, "while you were gone I was doing some thinking, and I have a proposition for you."

"A proposition?" Her eyes lit with interest. "Are we talking about a job here?"

"In a sense." He hesitated, then plunged ahead. "Are you serious about paying me back?"

"Yes," she said immediately.

God, he hadn't been this nervous since the first day he'd stood in front of the assembled employees of his father's company for the first time. "I could use your help with something," he said slowly.

Faith's gaze searched his expression, clearly looking for clues. "You need my help?"

He nodded. Then he took a deep breath and leaned forward. "I need a wife."

She stared at him, apparently sure she hadn't heard him correctly. He couldn't blame her. As soon as the words were out, he'd decided he was crazy. "You need *what?*"

"A wife." He could hear the embarrassment and impatience in his tone and he forced himself to take deep, slow breaths. Calming breaths.

She spread her hands in confusion and her smooth brow wrinkled in bewilderment. "But how can I help you with that? I doubt I know anyone who—"

"Faith." His deep voice stopped her tumbling words. "I'd like *you* to be my wife."

Her eyes widened. Her mouth formed a perfect O of surprise. She put a hand up and pointed to herself as if she needed confirmation that she hadn't lost her mind, and her lips soundlessly formed the word, "Me?"

He nodded, feeling an unaccustomed heat rising into his face. "Yes. You."

Two

Stone couldn't have shocked her more if he'd asked her to stand and start stripping. Faith stared at him, convinced he'd lost his mind.

"Not," he said hastily, "a *real* wife. Let me explain." He took a deep breath. He was looking down at his drink instead of at her, and she was surprised to see a dull bronze flush rising in his cheeks. "My mother is beginning to think about retirement. She's offered me her company, but before she'll turn it over she wants me to be married."

"Why would she do that?" She was completely baffled. What kind of mother would put her own child in a position like that?

"She thinks I need to settle down and give her some grandchildren." He snorted. "Although I can't imagine why. She's not exactly the most maternal person in the world."

She wondered if he heard the note of resentment and what else? Longing, perhaps, for something that hadn't been, in his voice. "Forcing you into marriage seems a little…extreme," she said carefully.

His face was grim. "My mother's a control freak. This is just one more little trick she's playing to try to arrange my life to suit herself." He bared his teeth in what she felt sure he thought was a smile. "So this time I intend to outfox her."

"What happens if you refuse to get married?"

He shrugged. "I guess she liquidates or sells. I didn't ask." He leaned forward, his eyes blazing a brilliant blue in the candlelight. "It would mean a lot to me, Faith. I want to keep Smythe Corp. a Lachlan holding."

"Why?"

He stared at her, clearly taken aback. "Why?" When she nodded, he sat back, as if to distance himself from the question. "Well, because it's a good business decision."

"But surely there are other companies out there that fit the bill. Why *this* company?"

"Because it's my heritage. My great-grandfather founded Smythe Corp. It would be a shame to see it pass out of the family."

There was something more there, she realized as she registered the tension in his posture, something she couldn't put her finger on, that underlay his stated reasons for wanting that particular company. But she had a feeling he wouldn't take kindly to being pushed any further.

"Will you do it?" he asked.

"I don't know." She chewed her lip. "It seems so dishonest—"

"Any less dishonest than trying to force me into marriage just because she's decreed it's time?" he demanded. For the first time, his control slipped and she caught a glimpse of the desperation lurking beneath his stoic facade. But he quickly controlled it, and when he spoke, his voice was calm again. "It would only be for a year," he said, "or a bit more. Strictly temporary. Strictly platonic. Except that we'd have to convince my mother that it's a real marriage. I'm not asking you to lie about anything that would hurt anyone." He stared deep into her eyes. "Think about that company, Faith. It's been in my family for three generations. If it's sold to an outsider, who knows what kind of restructuring might occur? Hundreds of people might lose their jobs."

She frowned at him. "That's emotional blackmail."

He grinned ruefully. "Did it work?"

She stared at him, her thoughts crashing over each other in chaotic patterns. "Would we live together?"

He nodded. "You'd have to move into my place for the duration. But we'd get an annulment when the time comes. And I'd expect to pay you for your time."

Pay you. She was almost ashamed of the mercenary thoughts that rushed through her head. Practical, she told herself, not mercenary. Not much. She couldn't possibly let him pay her. Not after all he'd done for her. This would be a good way to do something for him in return. Besides, if she moved in with him, she wouldn't have to keep renting her apartment.

She could go back to school, get a lot farther along in her education more quickly, if she didn't have living expenses. She only had a year and a half to go. Which meant that she'd be able to start repaying him sooner. Because regardless of what he said, she *was* going to pay back everything he'd done for her and her mother in the years since her father had died. And suddenly, that goal didn't seem so totally out of reach.

A profound relief washed over her and she closed her eyes for a moment.

"Are you all right?" He reached across the table and cupped her chin in his hand.

She swallowed, very aware of the warmth of his strong fingers on her skin. His touch sent small sizzling streamers of excitement coursing through her and she suppressed a shiver of longing. "Yes." But it came out a whisper. She cleared her throat. "But you can't pay me."

He released her chin, his brows snapping together. "Of course I'll—"

"No. I'm in your debt already."

"All right," he said promptly. "How about this: if you marry me for the time I need to get Smythe Corp., I'll consider all the debt you imagine you owe me to be paid in full."

She froze for a moment as hope blossomed. Then she realized she couldn't possibly make a deal like that. It wouldn't be fair to him. She started to shake her head, but before she could speak, Stone raised a hand.

"Hear me out. Marriage would be a sacrifice. You'd lose a year of your freedom. You'd be expected to attend social functions with me and play the part of hostess when we entertain. We'd have to convince my mother it was a real marriage for real reasons.''

She didn't ask what he meant, but she could feel a blush heating her own face now as she sat silently considering his proposal.

"It's a fair deal," he urged. "An exchange of favors, if you like."

She wasn't so sure of that. Taking care of her mother and her for eight years weighed a lot more on her scale than one measly year of marriage did. But when she met his gaze, she could see the iron determination there. If she didn't agree to this, he was liable to start in about paying her again.

And there was another factor, one that outweighed even her concerns about her finances. A moment ago, she'd seen naked panic in his eyes at the thought of losing that company. It wasn't financial, she was sure. But it was terribly important to Stone for some reason. And because she'd discerned that, she knew what her answer had to be.

"All right," she said hoarsely. "It's a deal. But there are three conditions."

He only raised one eyebrow.

"I'd like to continue with my education—"

"You don't need to finish school." Impatience quivered in every line of his big body. "You'll be doing me an enormous favor with this marriage. The least I can do is settle a sum on you at the end of the year. You won't need to work at all."

"I *want* to work," she insisted. "And I want to go back to school."

"You won't be able to work," he said. "Can you imagine what the press would do with that?"

Unfortunately she could. As one of the richest men

in the country, Stone dealt with a ridiculous amount of intrusive press.

"You'd have to consider being my wife your job," he said. "But I'll pay your tuition if you insist on taking classes."

"I do," she said firmly. "I'll reenroll for the summer session."

"All right. Now what's the third thing?"

She hated that she had to ask him for help with anything, but she had no choice. And it wasn't for her. "My mother," she said quietly. "The cost of her care—"

"Is not a problem for me," he said firmly. Then he leaned forward. "In fact, if you like, we could move your mother into my home. There's an apartment on the main floor for live-in help but I've never had anyone live in. She could stay there."

It was a generous offer and a generous thought, even if he was doing it for selfish reasons. She swallowed, more tempted by the thought than she should be. It would make her life much easier in many ways. And she'd be able to see her mother every day, perhaps even help with her care

"Please," Stone said. "I'd really like you to do this, Faith."

She studied his handsome face, serious and unsmiling, his eyes intense with the force of his will and an odd feeling rippled through her. "All right," she said. Then she cleared her throat and spoke more firmly. "I'll marry you."

The next morning, Saturday, he picked her up in his silver Lexus and took her to his home so that she could see where she'd be living and check out the apartment for her mother. He'd asked her to stop working immediately, and though he could tell she didn't like it, she'd informed him when he picked her up that she was no longer employed.

"Don't think of it as unemployed," he advised. "You just switched jobs."

She was silent as he maneuvered the car through Manhattan's insanely crowded streets to the quieter area where he made his home.

He could see her chewing her lip as she had the night before and he wondered what she was thinking. Worrying, probably, about whether or not she'd made a bad decision.

As he braked for a light, he said, "Thank you. I know this isn't an easy thing for you to do." He put his hand over hers where it lay in her lap and squeezed. This time he was prepared for the sensation her soft flesh aroused. Or so he told himself. Still, the shock he'd absorbed when he'd touched her last night reverberated through him. All he'd done was place his hand beneath her chin, letting his fingers rest against the silken skin of her cheek.

He thought he'd steeled himself for the same reaction that had hit him yesterday when he'd touched her lip.

But he hadn't been prepared for the strong current of attraction that tore through him, making him want to deepen the skin-to-skin contact in a very basic way. It was as if she was a live circuit and touching her plugged him in to her special current. He mentally shook his head. What was he doing, asking the girl to live in his home? Putting temptation right under his nose probably wasn't the smartest thing he'd ever done.

Still, as he drew her from the car and took the elevator from the garage to his Fifth Avenue town house across from Central Park, he felt an immense relief. Faith had been sheltered her entire life. Who knew what kind of things might happen to a naive girl like her on her own? He'd promised his father's memory that he'd take care of Faith, and he would.

Unlocking the door, he ushered her into his home. Inside the door, Faith stopped in the large central foyer, looking around. Though she'd spent her early years in a family that wanted for little, he imagined that the place seemed luxurious compared to the seedy little apartment in which she was living. Looking at it through her eyes, he watched her as he realized he was holding his breath waiting for her reaction.

"This is lovely," she said quietly. "Simply lovely."

He smiled, relieved. Straight ahead of them, a hallway led to the back of the house while a staircase just to the right of the hall climbed graciously to a landing that led to an upper floor. To the left was a formal living room with an equally formal dining room through an archway behind it; to their right was Stone's office, with its masculine desk, lined shelves of books and office equipment that filled the surfaces of the built-in counters along one wall.

"I'm glad you like it." He stepped around her and indicated the stairs. "Would you like to see the upstairs? I'll show you your room."

She moved obediently in the direction he indicated, climbing the stairs as he followed. He took her down the hallway past an open set of double doors, pausing briefly to indicate the masculine-looking master suite done in striking shades of burgundy, black and gold. "That's my room." Turning, he pointed to the doors just opposite. "And across the hall is a guest suite. Your room will be the next one on the right. It should suit you. It belonged to my mother years ago and I've never changed it." He shook his head. "She may have her flaws but I can't fault her taste."

Leading her to her room, he pushed open both doors.

"Oh," she said on a sigh, "it's *perfect.*"

It was a charming, feminine suite decorated in soft lavenders and blues accented with pure white. Though it was slightly smaller than his, it was still spacious, with a walk-in closet, a sitting area and a large full bath. He walked past her into the bathroom. "Our rooms are connected," he told her, sliding back a large set of louvered doors to reveal his bath and bedroom beyond. "No one will have to know we don't share a room."

She couldn't look him in the eye. "All right," she said in a muffled tone.

"Faith." He waited patiently until finally, she gazed across the room at him. "This will be a good arrangement for both of us. I promise to respect your privacy."

She nodded. Her cheeks had grown pink and he knew that she understood that he was telling her, in as gentle a way as he could, that she had nothing to fear from him sexually. No, appealing as she might be, he had no intention of changing the platonic status of their relationship.

By the time they had finished the house tour, it was lunchtime. He'd decided to show her how it would be when they lived together so he took her into the kitchen and seated her on a stool at the large island while he made tuna salad, sliced tomatoes and piled the combination between two halves of a croissant with cheese. He grilled the sandwiches while he sliced up a fresh pineapple.

"I didn't expect you to know your way around a kitchen," she told him, filling two glasses with ice and water as he'd asked her to do.

He grinned. "Figured I'd have a chef on standby waiting to fulfill my every wish?"

"Something like that." She glanced up at him and smiled. "I can cook, although I'm no Julia Child. I'd be happy to do the cooking."

"Actually," he admitted, "I do have a woman who comes in Monday through Thursday unless I have to be away. Why don't we keep her for the time being until you see how much free time you're going to have?"

"I'll have free time from nine-to-five every day of the week," she said. "If there's anything I can help with, all you have to do is ask."

He couldn't imagine asking her to get involved in any of his business dealings except in a social fashion, and he had someone to clean the house, so he couldn't think of anything he'd want her to do. "You'll have studying to do as soon as the summer term starts," he said instead. "And you'll be able to spend some time with your mother."

She brightened, and he remembered her pleasure last night at the idea of spending time with her mother. It was ironic, really, that they both had been deprived of their mothers for part of their childhoods. The difference was, she looked forward to spending precious time with her mother while he went out of his way to avoid close contact with his. "That will be nice." Her light voice broke into the dark thought. "We haven't had a lot of time together since I went away to school."

Which was not long after the accident in which their fathers had died, he thought, as an awkward silence fell.

"Sometimes it doesn't seem possible that Daddy's been gone for eight years." Her voice, quiet and subdued, broke the moment.

A stab of grief sharper than any he'd allowed himself to feel in a long time pierced his heart. "I know what you mean. Sometimes I still expect mine to walk through the door."

Her gaze flew to his. "This was your childhood home?"

He nodded. "Dad and Mother lived here when they were first married. After the divorce, she moved out."

"That must have been hard," she offered. "How old were you?"

"Six. And no, it wasn't particularly hard." He willed away the memories of his youth, of the nights he'd spent crying into his pillow, wondering what he'd done to make his mother leave. Of the days he'd envied schoolmates who had had mothers who cared enough to show up for visitors' days and school plays, mothers who sat in the stands during baseball games and cheered, mothers who planned birthday parties and actually remembered cake and presents. "My mother was rarely here and when she was, she and Dad were shouting the walls down half the time."

The sympathy shining in her silvery eyes moved him more than he wanted to admit. "My childhood was just the opposite. Extremely quiet. My mother's illness was diagnosed when I was less than two years old, and my father and I did our best to keep her from getting upset about anything." She rested her elbows on the bar and crossed her arms. "In that respect, we have something in common. I went to my dad with my problems, because I couldn't go to my mother."

He smiled. "Did you know I used to go to the Mets games with your father and mine?" He shook his head. "Dad had great seats right along the third base line and we never missed a home game. Those two knew every player's stats going back to the beginning of time. And they used to argue about who the MVP was each season, who should go to the All-Star team, who ought to be traded…looking back, I think they just argued because it was fun."

Her eyes were crinkled in laughter. "I've never heard about this before." Her smile faded slightly, wobbled. "I guess you probably have a lot of memories of my father that I don't."

He hesitated, torn between lying to spare her feelings and telling her the truth. Truth won. "Yeah, I guess I do. Some of my best memories are of times I spent with my dad and yours. I'll tell you some more when we have time." He rose and took the lunch plates to the sink for the housekeeper. "This afternoon, I'd like to go pick out rings. Is that all right with you?"

Her gray eyes widened. "Rings? Is that really necessary?"

He nodded, a little disappointed that she didn't yet

seem to grasp the seriousness of his proposal. "Yes. This will be a real marriage, Faith." He almost reached for her shoulders, then stopped himself, remembering the desire that had knocked him over the last time he'd touched her. "Our reasons might be a little different from most people's but we'll be as legally wed as the next couple. So let's go get rings."

He called ahead, so that they would have some privacy while they shopped, and thirty minutes later, he handed her out of a cab in front of Tiffany & Company. Faith was a quiet presence at his side as they waited for the doors to be unlocked.

As they stepped into the cool hush of the store, a beaming saleswoman was upon them. "Welcome, Mr. Lachlan. It is Tiffany's pleasure and mine to serve you. How can we help you today?"

"Wedding rings," he said.

The woman's eyes widened as did those of the other employees ranged behind her, and he wondered how many minutes it would be until the press got wind of his marriage. He supposed he should warn Faith, though certainly she knew how ridiculously newsworthy his life was. Then he realized that they had better each tell their mothers about their plans before they read it in tomorrow's paper.

"We have a lovely selection right back here." The saleswoman had recovered quickly and was indicating that they should follow her.

Twenty minutes later, Faith was still perched on the edge of a comfortable chair, quietly staring at the array of precious stones scattered across the black velvet before her. She shook her head. "I couldn't possibly—"

From where he stood behind her, Stone said, "All

right. If you can't decide, I'll choose one." He knew she'd been going to say something ridiculous, like, "I couldn't possibly accept such an expensive ring when you've already done so much for me." It bothered him that the salespeople hovering around with their antennae primed for gossip would find rich pickings if they knew the truth about this marriage. Only, of course, because he couldn't risk having his mother find out. Of course.

He bent down to Faith and murmured in her ear. "Be careful what you say in here—it will get into the papers."

That startled her, he could tell by the way she jerked around and stared up at him, her face wearing an expression of shock. While she was still staring at him, he reached for a stunning square, brilliant-cut diamond ring with progressively smaller diamonds trailing down each side. It was set in platinum. He'd liked it the moment the woman had pulled it out of the case, and he suspected Faith liked it, too, from the way her eyes had caressed it. He lifted her left hand from her lap and immediately felt the tingling electricity that arced between them as their flesh connected. He took a deep breath and slipped the ring onto her third finger. There was just a hint of resistance at the knuckle before it slid smoothly into place and he quickly dropped her hand as if it burned. It was the same feeling he'd convinced himself he hadn't felt when he'd taken her chin in his hand, indeed when he touched her in any way.

"A perfect fit." He caught her gaze, forcing himself to behave as if nothing out of the ordinary had happened. "Do you like this one?"

"It's…" She shrugged, lifting dazed eyes to his. "It's beautiful," she whispered.

"Good." He studied the way her long, elegant fingers set off the ring, a deep satisfaction spreading through him. His ring. His wife. He was surprised at how much he liked the thought. Maybe this year wouldn't be such a trial at all, with Faith at his side. The more he thought about Faith and marriage, the better he realized his solution was. She could protest all she liked, but he would set up a trust fund for her and her mother so that once this arrangement ended she wouldn't be afraid of where her next meal would come from or how her mother's next medical bill would be paid.

He turned her hand and linked his fingers through hers. To the saleswoman, he said, "We'll take the matching wedding bands."

"Stone!"

"Faith!" he teased. "Did you think I was going to let you get away without a wedding band?"

The saleswoman had flown off in a twitter to get the proper ring sizes. He followed her across the room, catching her attention and motioning for quiet. "I'd also like the sapphire-and-diamond choker and matching earrings in the display window. But don't let my fiancée see them."

The woman's eyes got even wider. "Very good, Mr. Lachlan. And may I congratulate you on your engagement, sir."

"Thank you," he replied, resigned to the fact that tomorrow's paper would carry a mention of his upcoming wedding. His only consolation was that it would take them a day or two before they figured out who the bride-to-be was. "I'd like you to deliver the wedding rings and the sapphire set to my home. She'll wear the engagement ring.''

He called his mother the moment they got back into a cab. She wasn't available so he told her assistant that he'd gotten engaged that afternoon and that he'd like her to come for dinner and meet his bride Saturday evening, and hung up.

Within thirty seconds, the cell phone rang. He chuckled as he punched the speaker button on the phone. ''Hello, Mother.''

''Was that a joke?'' Eliza Smythe demanded.

''Not in the least.'' He kept his tone pleasant. ''We'd like you to come to dinner tonight to make her acquaintance.''

''So I don't know her?'' The tone was exasperated.

''You know of her, I believe,'' he replied. ''Faith Harrell. She's the daughter of—''

''Randall.'' His mother's tone was softer. ''He was a good man. I was so sorry when he—good Lord!'' she said suddenly. ''Stone, that girl isn't even legal! Are you crazy?''

''Faith will be twenty-one this year,'' he said coolly.

''All right.'' Eliza Smythe changed tactics abruptly. ''I'll come to dinner. I can't wait to meet Miss Harrell.''

''She'll be Mrs. Lachlan soon,'' he reminded her. ''Why don't we say seven o'clock? See you then.''

She couldn't stop staring at the engagement ring. It was breathtaking, the central stone over three carats. He'd paid an obscene amount of money for it, she was sure, though no one on the Tiffany staff had been indiscreet enough to actually mention payment in front of her. She had noticed Stone placing a hasty phone call to his insurance agent, so at least if she left it lying in the ladies' room somewhere it would be covered.

Not that she ever intended to take it off her finger.

She was so preoccupied that when Stone opened the cab door and put a hand beneath her elbow, she looked up at him in confusion. "Where are we going now?"

"Shopping." He helped her from the car. "You probably need some things for the formal occasions we'll be going to from time to time. Next weekend, we'll attend a charity ball. That will give everyone an opportunity to hear about our marriage and gawk at you. After that, things should settle down."

A charity ball? She'd never had any experience with such things although her family had been modestly wealthy—unless you compared them to Stone, in which case they didn't even register on the personal fortune scale.

"Um, no, that would be fine," she said. "I suppose the sooner the news of this gets out, the sooner the fuss will die down."

He glanced down at her. "I'm sorry if the thought of the media unnerves you. I generally don't do much that excites them. This will make a splash but it'll fade the minute there's a scandal or someone bigger crosses their sights."

She shook her head, smiling at him pityingly. "You underestimate your appeal."

He grinned at her, so handsome and confident her heart skipped a beat. "You'll see." Then his face sobered. "I'd like to get married soon," he said.

"Well, it shouldn't take long to get things organized," she said. If the mere thought of marrying him unnerved her like this, how was she going to get through the real thing? "I'm assuming you don't want to make a fuss of this wedding so we probably could get it together in three months—"

"Faith."

She stopped.

"If I apply for the license tomorrow we could be married on Thursday or Friday."

She blinked, shook her head to clear her ears. "*Next* Friday?"

"Mmm-hmm."

"But how can we possibly...never mind." She smiled feebly. "I guess you have people who can arrange these things."

He nodded. "I do. Do you prefer a church or the courthouse?"

"Courthouse," she said hastily. Getting married in a church would feel sacrilegious, when they had no intention of honoring the vows they would be taking. A dull sense of disappointment spread through her, and she gave herself a mental shake.

"All right." As far as he was concerned, the matter appeared to be settled. "Then let's go get you a wedding dress."

"Oh, I don't need—" She felt as if she'd hopped a train only to find it racing along at top speed, skipping its regular stops.

"Yes," he said positively. "You do."

Shopping with Stone was an education. *More like a nightmare,* she thought, suppressing a smile as he fired orders at a salesperson. She tried repeatedly to tell him she didn't need all these clothes; he rolled

right over her objections. She supposed she should
be grateful for small mercies. At least he hadn't followed her into the dressing room or insisted she
model for him.

He dragged her from one shop to the next. Neiman
Marcus, Barney's, the new Celine flagship store. For
day, a short black Prada, a Celine herringbone suit
and a striking black-and-pink Cavalli blouse with
Red Tape jeans. Everywhere they went, he was recognized sooner or later. She could tell exactly when
it happened from the appraising looks that began to
fly her way. For the first time, it occurred to her that
marrying Stone might change her life forever. He
was a public figure and without a doubt, she would
become one for the duration of their marriage. But
would she be able to resume her normal anonymous
lifestyle after they parted?

"We'll take all three of those gowns she liked,"
he said, oblivious to the direction of her thoughts as
he nodded at the fawning saleswomen.

"All three" included an Emanuel Ungaro sea-
foam-green silk mousseline wrap dress with a halter
collar, no back and a slit clear up her thigh, a strapless Escada with a fitted, silver-embroidered bodice
and a full, Cinderella-like skirt with tulle underlayers
in silver and blue, and a classic black organza with
laser-cut trim by Givenchy.

And there were shoes. Walter Steiger pumps for
the day dresses. Sergio Rossi mules in black for the
jeans. Silver heels from Ferretti, a pair of Jimmy
Choo Swarovski crystal-and-satin slip-ons in the
same soft green as one of the dresses. And for the
classic black, equally classic open-toe Versace heels.
All with matching bags.

It was mind-boggling, she thought, as he hustled her back into the car after the final store. When Stone made a decision, he didn't let time lapse before carrying out his plans. It might be something to remember.

It was actually a relief to see the sturdy stone facade of her soon-to-be residence appear. Stone's home overlooking Central Park was everything she'd expected the first time she'd seen it that morning. And more. Much more. Brass and glass. Modern cleverly blended with antique. Fresh flowers and thriving potted plants. Understated elegance.

At his direction, all of their recent purchases had been sent to his home since, as he pointed out, they'd simply have to move them again when she moved in. When they arrived, everything had been delivered and the housekeeper had it all piled in Faith's room.

Her room. She couldn't believe she would be living here with him, *sleeping* just one room away from him, in only a few days. Since they didn't have a lot of time, she'd brought over what she would need for this evening's dinner with his mother and planned to change there.

"I'll meet you back down here in…forty-five minutes?" Stone was consulting his watch. "That will give us a few minutes to relax before my mother arrives."

His mother. Her stomach jumped as she nodded and went to her room. She'd never met Eliza Smythe and knew only what she'd read in the news about the hard-hitting, hardworking female who had taken over Smythe Corp. after her father's unexpected death from a heart attack at a young age. She took deep breaths and tried to settle the nerves that arose at the thought of being vetted by the woman. What if his mother didn't like her?

Three

———

She was right on the button when she descended the steps a few minutes after he did. Stone, in the act of entering the drawing room, glanced up—and froze where he was.

Faith wore what at first glance appeared to be a simple dress in a lightweight Black Watch plaid. But a second glance at her figure in the soft brushed fabric dispelled any doubt that this was a demure dress for the classroom or office. She wore the collar open and turned up, framing a long, delicate neck and fragile collarbone, and her hair was up in a classic, shining twist. A matching fabric belt encircled her slender waist. The sleeves were three-quarter-length and tiny buttons ran from a point between her breasts to midthigh, allowing a slight glimpse of smooth, slim leg as she came down the stairs.

And as he realized that those thighs were encased

in black fishnet stockings and incredibly well-displayed in a pair of the new heels they'd just bought, his blood pressure shot straight through the roof. He'd never thought he was a leg man, but he sure wasn't having much success keeping his mind off Faith's legs. Or any of her other perfectly rounded feminine attributes, either, for that matter.

"You look very…nice," he said, and then winced at the banality.

But she smiled. "Good. I know your mother will be coming straight from the office and I thought this would work better than something that's really for evening. It's a Ralph Lauren," she added smugly. "I got it at a secondhand shop for a pittance!"

He grinned. She hadn't realized yet that cost was a concept she no longer needed to consider. "Would you like a drink?"

She hesitated. "I'm not really much of a drinker. A glass of wine, perhaps?"

"How about champagne? Since we are celebrating our engagement." He gestured for her to precede him into the drawing room, which gave him a chance to scrutinize the back view of her dress. Yeow. It was a good thing this marriage wasn't for real. He could imagine getting overly possessive at the thought of other men putting their hands on her, even in a correct public dance position.

Duh. What was he thinking about that for? Wasn't going to happen. Was. Not. Besides, he reminded himself, he shouldn't be ogling her, either. She was his ward.

The caterer he'd hired had set out an assortment of hors d'oeuvres on a table in a corner. A small flame beneath a silver chafing dish kept some crab balls warm, and around it, a selection of fruits, vegetables and a paté with crackers made an attractive display.

"Pretty," she commented, picking up a strawberry and biting into it. "I've never had champagne. Will I like it?"

"Probably, if you like wine," he said, crossing to the bar where an ice bucket contained a tall-necked French bottle. Watching the way she savored the luscious red fruit, the way her lips had closed around the morsel as her eyelids fluttered down in unconscious ecstasy, he was uncomfortably aware of the stirring pulses of arousal that threatened to turn his trousers into an article of torture. He might be her guardian but he was also a human male...with a healthy sexual appetite. And right now, he was hungry for *her*. Hastily he turned away and poured a glass of the pale golden sparkling liquid for her and one for himself.

Taking a deep breath and reaching for self-control, he came to where she stood in the middle of the room. He handed her one flute and held his aloft in a toast. "To a successful partnership."

"To a successful partnership," she repeated, lifting her gaze to his as their glasses sounded a pure chime and they each lifted them to drink. Their eyes met and held for a moment before she looked away, a warm pink blush rising in her cheeks.

He watched her over the rim of his glass as she tasted her first champagne. Her eyes widened slightly as she inhaled the fruity fragrance, and then she promptly sneezed as the bubbles tickled her nose.

"Bless you," he said, laughing, glad for the distraction. "You have to watch that."

"It's delicious," she said, taking an experimental sip. Then she slanted a flirtatious smile at him from beneath her lashes. "Is this one of the benefits of being married to a millionaire?"

He felt his whole body tighten in reaction to that teasing smile. He was sure she had no idea what that smile made a man want to do, and he forced himself to ignore the urge to reach out and pull her against him to erase it with his mouth. "This is one of the benefits of being married to a man who likes a good wine,' he said. "Listen, we need to talk a little bit before my mother arrives."

"About what?" She held her glass very correctly by the stem and he was reminded that although she didn't have a lot of money, she'd grown up in a very genteel home and a carefully selected school which had only enhanced her ladylike ways.

"My mother," he said carefully, "has to be convinced that we married for…the reasons normal couples get married."

He watched as she processed that. "You mean you want me to pretend to be in love with you," she pronounced.

"Uh, right." He'd expected some coy reaction, not such a straightforward response, and he forced himself to acknowledge that a corner of his pride might be dented just the smallest bit. She appeared completely unaffected by the idea of being in love with him. That was good, he assured himself, since that particular emotion would royally foul up their arrangement for the coming year.

"Okay."

"Okay? It might not be easy," he warned, dragging his mind back to the topic. "She's going to walk in here in a foul temper. So just follow my lead.''

"Yes, o master.'' She smiled as she took another sip of her drink.

He took her glass of champagne and set it firmly aside, guiding her to the food. ''Get yourself a bite to eat. The last thing I need is for you to be silly with drink when my mother arrives.''

"I've only had half a glass," she said serenely. But she allowed him to spread paté on a cracker and lift it to her mouth. She leaned forward and opened her lips, closing them around a portion of the cracker, crunching cleanly into it with straight white teeth. Her lips brushed his fingers, closed briefly over the very tip of one, and then withdrew.

And he realized immediately he'd made a monumental mistake. The sensation of her warm, slick mouth on him brought erotic images to flood his brain and his body stirred with a powerful surge of sensual intensity. Hastily he stepped back, hoping she hadn't noticed his discomfort. His fingers were wet from her lips and he almost lifted them to his own mouth before he realized what he was doing. Wiping them on a napkin, he tried desperately to fix his thoughts on something, anything other than the unconscious sensuality that his ward—his wife, soon—wore like other women wore perfume.

She chewed the bite for a time, then licked her lips. ''That's excellent!''

Watching her pink tongue delicately flick along the outer corner of her mouth, he couldn't agree more. God, she was driving him crazy.

Faith was practically a sister to him, he reminded himself sternly. This was merely a business type of arrangement from which they both would benefit. He'd fulfill his mother's wishes, in his own fashion and get Smythe Corp. Faith could finish her education, which she seemed determined to do. And it had the added benefit of making her feel as if she was paying him back, of divesting herself of the debt she imagined she owed him for the years he'd taken care of her and her mother.

Yes, it was going to be a good arrangement. And if he couldn't stop his overactive imagination from leaping straight to thoughts of what it would be like to have her writhing beneath him in a big, soft bed, at least he could keep her from knowing it.

The doorbell rang then and he glanced at his watch. His mother, ever-punctual. "Brace yourself," he warned Faith as he started for the foyer. "I'll let her in."

Faith looked up from the grape she was about to eat. "Surely she isn't that bad."

He merely raised one eyebrow.

The doorbell rang again, impatiently, and she made a shooing motion as she set down her plate. "Go! Let her in. And be nice."

Be nice. He snorted with amusement as he walked to the massive front door and twisted the knob. Like his mother had ever needed anyone to be nice to her. She'd probably steamroll them right into the pavement as she moved past.

"Good evening, Mother." He stepped aside and ushered in the petite woman whose dark hair was still the same shade as his own, with the added distinction of a few silver streaks at her temples.

"Hello." His mother whipped off her gloves and coat and thrust them unceremoniously into his arms as she stalked in. "Would you care to explain to me exactly what you think you're doing?"

"Excuse me?" He deliberately infused his tone with innocence.

Eliza made a rude noise. "Where's this woman you've talked into marrying you? And how much did you have to pay her?"

"I didn't pay her anything." That was absolutely true, so far. "My bride-to-be is in the drawing room." He indicated the archway and his mother strode forward.

As Eliza entered the drawing room, he hastily disposed of her outerwear and followed her. Faith came across the room as they appeared, her hand extended. For a moment, he couldn't take his eyes off her. She wore a welcoming smile that looked too genuine to be faked, and her slender body moved gracefully beneath the soft fabric of the fitted dress.

"Hello, Ms. Smythe," she said, her gray eyes warm. "It's a pleasure to meet you."

The older woman took her hand and Stone watched her give Faith a firmer than necessary handshake. "I wish I could say the same," she said coolly. "What did my son promise you for going through with this ridiculous charade?"

Faith's eyes widened. Shock filled them, then he could see the distress rush in. "I, uh, we—"

"Mother." He spoke sharply, diverting her attention from Faith. "You can either be courteous to my fiancée in my home or you can leave. You should have no trouble remembering the way out," he added, unable to prevent the acid edge to the words.

His mother had the grace to flush. "Please forgive my rudeness," she said to Faith, sounding like she

meant it. Then she turned one gimlet eye on her son.
"But I believe this hasty union was arranged for the
purpose of circumventing my wishes in regard to an
offer I made my son."

"How could you possibly know why I want to
marry her?" he demanded. "You don't know enough
about my life to be making snap judgments."

"She's a child." His mother dismissed Faith with
one curt sentence. "I'm no fool, Stone. If you think
you're going to con me into believe—"

"I don't care what you believe." He put a hand
on Faith's back, feeling the rigid tension in every
muscle. Deliberately he slid his palm under her collar
to the smooth, bare flesh at her nape, gently massag-
ing the taut cords, his big hand curving possessively
around her slender neck. "Faith and I have known
each other since we both were children. I've been
waiting for her to grow up and she has. When you
made me your offer, I realized there was no reason
to wait anymore." He exerted a small amount of
pressure with his fingers, tugging Faith backward
against him. "Right, darling?"

She turned her head to look up at him and he could
see the uncertainty in the depths of her bottomless
gray eyes. "Right," she replied, her voice barely audible. Her face was white, probably from shock. He
doubted she'd ever had words with *her* mother that
were anything like this scene. She couldn't have
looked less like a thrilled bride-to-be, so he did the
only thing he could think of to make his case more
convincing: he kissed her.

As he bent his head and took her lips, he put his
arms around her and turned her to him, pulling her
unresisting frame close. The moment their lips met,

he felt that punch of desire in his diaphragm, a sensation he still hadn't gotten accustomed to. His head began to spin.

Her lips were soft and warm beneath his, and as he molded her mouth, she made a quiet murmur deep in her throat. The small sound set a match to his barely banked desire, and he slid his arms more fully around her, pressing her long, slender curves to him. Faith lifted her arms around his shoulders and as her gentle fingers brushed the back of his neck, he shuddered. The intimate action moved the sweet swell of her breasts across his chest and rational thought fled as he gathered her even closer.

"Good grief," his mother said. "You can stop now. You've convinced me."

It took him a moment to remember that they had an audience, to make sense of the words. Faith's mouth was soft and yielding, still clinging to his when he broke the kiss and dragged in a steadying breath of air. She kept her arms looped around his neck, her face buried in his throat, and as her warm breath feathered across his throat, his hands clenched spasmodically on her back with the effort it took him not to drag her into a private room to finish what they'd started.

Taking a deep breath, he forced his fingers to relax. He raised his head and looked at his mother over Faith's fair hair. "We weren't trying to convince you," he said roughly. And it was true. He might have started the kiss with that intent, but the moment Faith surrendered to the sensual need that enveloped him every time he touched her, he'd forgotten all about convincing anyone of anything.

Then Faith stirred in his arms, pushing against his

chest until he released her. She straightened her dress
and smoothed her hair, uttering a small laugh. "I
apologize if we made you uncomfortable," she said
to his mother. "When Stone kisses me like that, I
have a hard time remembering my name, much less
my manners or anything else." She turned to Stone
and her voice was steady although her eyes were still
soft and dazed. "I'm sure your mother would like a
drink, darling."

He had to force himself not to let his jaw drop.
She was a better actress than he'd expected, and his
own tense demeanor eased as he saw the suspicion
in his mother's eyes fade. "Will you join us in a
glass of champagne, Mother?" he asked her. "And
help us celebrate this special time?"

The rest of the evening went smoothly. He kept
Faith close to him, holding her hand or with his arm
loosely around her waist, most of the time when they
weren't at the table, not giving his mother any opportunity to corner her alone and harass her. It was
both heaven and hell to feel her warm curves at his
side, and he told himself he was only trying to convince his mother that their marriage was a love
match. But he couldn't quite ignore the leaping pleasure in every nerve ending. God, what he wouldn't
give to have the right to make her his wife in the
fullest sense of the word!

She had recovered her innate elegant manners by
the time they went in to dinner. And though she was
quiet, he imagined it was simply because he and his
mother were discussing business matters much of the
time.

Touching her, he decided as they settled on the
love seat in the drawing room again after the meal,

was like a damned drug. Addictive. He had his arm around her and he idly smoothed his thumb over the ball of her shoulder joint as his mother turned to her and said, "Faith, I hope you'll forgive my earlier behavior. Welcome to the family."

Faith smiled. "Thank you."

"Faith's mother will be moving in with us soon." He didn't know why he was telling his mother this, but he plowed on. "She suffers from multiple sclerosis and we're fixing up an apartment for her on the main floor."

Eliza turned to Faith. "I never met your mother. Has she had MS long?"

"Almost all my life," Faith responded, her smile fading. "I was a late baby and she was diagnosed just over a year later. But I think she had symptoms years before that and ignored them."

His mother nodded. "My first secretary, who was absolutely invaluable during the first years when I stepped into my father's shoes, was diagnosed when she was forty-four. It was terribly difficult to watch her slowly lose capabilities. She passed away last year." Her eyes brimmed with tears; he was amazed. He'd never seen his mother cry, had never even imagined that she could. Which, he supposed, was a sad indicator of the degree to which they'd stayed out of each other's lives. Still, she was the one who had initiated the estrangement, if it could even be called that. There was no reason for him to feel guilty about it.

At his side, Faith stirred and he realized she was passing his mother a cocktail napkin so she could wipe her eyes. "It *is* difficult to accept that there's so little we can do to combat it," she said. "After my father died, my mother's condition worsened rapidly.''

After a few more moments of conversation, Eliza set down her drink and rose. "Call me a taxi, please, Stone. It's time for me to be going.''

He did so, then helped her on with her coat and they stood in the foyer for a few moments until the car rolled down the street and stopped in front of the house.

As he closed the door behind her, he turned to Faith, still standing at his side in the foyer. "We did it! We convinced her.'' He took her hands, squeezing lightly. "Thank you.''

"You're welcome.'' She smiled slightly but he noticed her gaze didn't reach any higher than his chin as she eased her hands free of his and turned. "It's been a tiring day. Could you take me home now?''

"Of course.'' His elation floated away, leaving him feeling flat and depressed. And there was no reason for it, he told himself firmly. He'd accomplished what he'd intended. So what if he had a raging physical attraction to Faith? She wasn't indifferent to him, either. He was certain of it after that smoking kiss before dinner, but she clearly wasn't any more prepared to step over the line than he was.

And he knew he should be glad for that. Because if she encouraged him, he was fairly certain he'd forget he'd ever drawn that line in the first place.

Faith spent the following Monday packing most of her things and answering breathless questions from Gretchen about her upcoming marriage. The morning paper had carried a tantalizing mention of Stone's impending nuptials and Gretchen had been quick to add up the details and come to the right conclusion.

Stone picked her up just after two o'clock and they made the drive into rural Connecticut where her mother lived in a beautifully landscaped condominium. Her apartment was on the ground floor and was handicap-accessible. Faith had helped her find the place during one of her infrequent vacations from school. Only now did it occur to her that Stone had probably helped her mother sell their old house. And rather than using it to finance this purchase, she was willing to bet he'd used it to pay off her father's debts and had spent his own money on her mother since then.

The thought of him assuming the full financial burden of caring for her mother and her still pricked at her pride, but she was grateful, too. She was practical enough to recognize that she never could have provided her mother with a stable, comfortable home. God only knew what would have become of them if Stone hadn't stepped in. What had her father been thinking?

They probably would never know. Her throat tightened as she thought of the laughing man with hair as pale as her own who had tossed her into the air and tucked her into bed every night. Clearly he hadn't been perfect, but she would always think of him with love.

Thank God, she thought again, for Stone. He'd provided desperately needed tranquillity for her mother and also had given Faith the tools to make her own way in the world one day. And she was all the more determined to repay his kindness during the upcoming year. She'd be such an asset to him he would wonder what he'd done before he had a wife! A momentary flash of disquiet accompanied the thought. Already, it was as though she'd been with Stone for months rather than days. What would it be like to lose him after a year?

Clarice, her mother's day help, answered the door when Stone rang the bell. "Hello, honey," the older woman greeted Faith. "She's really looking forward to your visit."

Faith hugged her. Clarice was a godsend. Widowed at sixty, Clarice had little in the way of retirement savings and was forced to continue to work. Faith and her mother had tried three other aides before they found Clarice, and Faith knew a gem when she saw one. Clarice, in addition, appeared to genuinely enjoy Mrs. Harrell and swore the work was well within her capabilities. Fortunately Faith's mother wasn't a large woman, so it wasn't terribly difficult for Clarice to assist her for tasks like getting in and out of the bath.

Still, Faith worried. Her mother was steadily losing mobility and motor control and the day was coming when she would need more than occasional assistance and handicapped facilities in her home. But as she entered the condo with Stone behind her, she felt less burdened, less worried than she had in some time. For the next year, her mother would want for nothing. And as soon as Faith got her degree and a job with decent pay, she planned to find a place she could share with her mother that would meet both their needs.

"Clarice," she said, "this is Stone Lachlan, my fiancé." She was proud that she didn't stumble over the word—she'd practiced it in her head fully half of the trip.

"Hello," said Clarice, "Faith's never brought—" Then the import of Faith's words struck her. "Well, my lands! Come in, come in. Congratulations!" She pumped Stone's hand, then hugged Faith. "Does your mother know?"

Faith shook her head. "Not yet. Is she in the living room?"

The older woman nodded. "By the window. She loves to look out at the birds. I put some feeders up to attract them and we've been seeing all kinds."

Faith felt another rush of gratitude. Clarice was indeed a gem. She wondered if there was any possibility of convincing her to come with her mother to live in New York. Deciding not to get ahead of herself, she let Clarice lead them into the living room.

"Mama." She went to the wheelchair by the window and knelt to embrace her mother, tears stinging her eyes.

"Hello, my little love." Her mother's arms fumbled up to pat at her. Her speech was slow but still reasonably clear, although Faith had noticed some change over the past year. Then her mother said, "Stone!"

"Hello, Mrs. Harrell." He came forward and Faith was surprised when he knelt at her side and gave her mother his hand. "It's nice to see you again."

"You, also." Naomi Harrell clung to his hand. "Did you drive Faith up?"

He nodded. Then he looked at Faith, and she smiled at him, grateful to him for sensing that she wanted to be the one to tell her mother of their marriage.

"Mama, I—we have some news. Stone and I are engaged to be married."

"Engaged?" Naomi slurred the second "g" and her eyes, magnified by the thick glasses she wore, went wide. "You're getting married?"

Stone looked at Faith again, still smiling, and for a moment, she was dizzied by the warm promise in his eyes, until she realized he was putting on a show for her mother's sake. "We are," he said. "This Friday, at eleven o'clock. We'd like you to be there, if you are able."

Naomi Harrell looked from one of them to the other. "I didn't even know you were dating," she said to Faith.

The comment shouldn't have caught her off guard but it did. "We, um, haven't been going out long," she said. Understatement of the year.

Stone slipped one steely arm around her shoulders, pulling her against his side. "I swept her off her feet," he told her mother, then turned again to smile down at her. "I was afraid if I waited until she was finished with school, the competition might edge me out." He paused, looking back at her mother. "I wasn't about to lose her."

Her mother nodded slowly, and Faith wasn't surprised to see tears welling in her eyes. Naomi Harrell had known that kind of love for real. She accepted the idea that her daughter had found the same happiness more easily than Stone's mother had. "I'm glad," Naomi said. "Faith needs somebody."

Faith knew her mother only meant that she didn't want Faith to be alone in the event anything happened to her. It was an upsetting thought. "That's not all, Mama," she said, anxious to get it all said and done. "Stone and I would like you to come and live with us after we're married. Stone has an apartment on the main floor of his home that you could have. There's plenty of room for you and Clarice, too, if she'd consider leaving this area."

But Naomi was shaking her head. "New-ly-weds," she said, enunciating carefully, "should have some time alone."

Stone chuckled. "Mrs. Harrell, my home is big enough for all of us. Your apartment can be completely self-contained. There's even an entrance from the back. You don't even have to see us if you don't want to."

Naomi smiled. "I want to. But I don't want to be in the way."

"Mama, I'd really, really love it if you'd come to live with me." Faith took her mother's hands. "I miss you."

"And besides," Clarice piped up, "this way we'll be right there when the grandbabies start arriving!"

Oh my Lord. If there was any way she could put those words back in Clarice's mouth...she felt herself begin to blush.

At her side, Stone stirred, bringing his other hand up to rest over hers and her mother's. "We aren't ready to think about that yet," he said. "I want Faith all to myself for a while. A long while."

"And besides," she added, "I have to finish school and get established in my career." Well, at least *that* wasn't a lie.

"Yes, I can't seem to talk her out of this obsession with working." Stone's voice was easy and colored with humor, but she sensed a grain of truth beneath the light tone. She was sure it wasn't her imagination. Thinking of the tension between him and his own mother, she wondered just how deeply he'd been scarred by his parents' split when he was a child.

She recalled the acid in his voice the night he'd suggested that his mother knew the way out—it had been a deliberate attempt to hurt. And judging from his mother's slight flinch before she controlled her expression, the shot had hit its mark. She felt badly for Eliza Smythe even though she didn't agree with the way she'd apparently put business before her young son more than two decades ago. Eliza's face had shown a heartbreaking moment of envy when Stone had told her about Faith's mother moving in with them. Again, she suspected he'd done it because he knew it would hurt. Or maybe he'd *hoped* it would, she thought with a sudden flash of insight. Children who had been rejected often continued to try to win their parent's attention, even in negative ways.

She sighed. She'd *liked* her new mother-in-law-to-be. Was it too much to hope that during her year with Stone she could contribute to mending the obvious rift between them?

Her year with Stone. As they said farewell to her mother and Clarice, Faith was conscious of the large warm shape of him at her side, one big hand gently resting in the middle of her back. He smelled like the subtle, but expensive, cologne he always wore, and abruptly she was catapulted back to Saturday night, when he'd taken her in his arms. That scent had enveloped her as he'd pulled her to him and kissed her.

He'd kissed her! She still thought it might have been a dream, except that she could recall his mother's wry, amused expression far too well. No wonder she'd been amused. For Faith, the world had changed forever the moment he'd touched her. And when his firm, warm lips had come down on hers and his arms had brought her against every muscled inch of his hard body, she'd forgotten everything but the wonderfully strange sensations rushing through her. Her body had begun to heat beneath his hands. She'd wanted more, although she didn't quite know what to do next to get it. But when she'd lifted her arms and circled his broad shoulders, the action had brushed her sensitive breasts against him and she'd wanted to *move,* to cuddle her body as close to his as she could get, to press herself against him even more. When he'd lifted his head, she'd simply hung in his arms as he'd spoken to his mother. God, the man was potent! She had been too embarrassed to face Eliza Smythe for a moment, then she'd simply told her the truth. She *did* forget everything when Stone kissed her.

Covertly she studied him from beneath her lashes. Stone's big hands looked comfortable and confident on the wheel of the Lexus and she shivered as she remembered the way they'd slid restlessly over her body as he'd kissed her. Would he do it again?

She wanted him to. Badly. In fact, she wanted far more than his kisses. She was almost twenty-one years old and she'd never even had a serious boyfriend. Soon she would have a husband. She studied his chiseled profile, the jut of his chin, the solid jaw, the way his hair curled just the smallest bit around his ears. She'd been half in love with him practically her whole life and being with him constantly over the past few days had only shown her how much more she could feel.

Quickly she turned her head and looked out the window before he could catch her staring at him like a lovesick fool. He didn't love her, only needed her for the most practical of reasons. But still…her heart was young and optimistic, unbruised and whole. He might not love her, but he certainly seemed to desire her. Wasn't that a start? Maybe, in time, if they got close…physically, he'd begin to need her the way she was realizing she needed him. It was too new to analyze. But she knew, with a not entirely pleasant certainty, that if she couldn't change his mind about making this a longer than one-year marriage, she wouldn't be able to leave him behind easily.

Not easily at all. In fact, she wasn't sure she could ever forget him. What man would ever measure up to Stone in her estimation?

She was afraid she knew the answer to that.

Four

Back in Manhattan, he headed home.

"Where are you going?" Faith asked.

He glanced across at her. She'd been very quiet the whole ride, apparently lost in her own thoughts. "Home."

"My home or your home?"

"Our home." He put a slight emphasis on the pronoun.

"It won't be our home until Friday," she said, using the same emphasis. "And I need to go to my apartment in any case. I still have things to pack."

"I can send someone to finish the job. We have things to do."

"I'd rather you didn't," she said mildly.

"It's no problem. And it will save you—"

"No, thank you." She shook her head, her blond hair flying and her tone was definite enough to warn him that he was traveling a narrow path here. "No. I would like to pack myself. There's not that much."

"Can I at least send someone to pick everything up and move it for you?"

She smiled, and a small dimple appeared in her soft cheek, enchanting him. "That would be nice. They could come Friday afternoon."

"Friday afternoon? Why not tomorrow? Surely you don't have that much stuff to move."

The smile had disappeared. "I'm not planning on moving in until after the ceremony on Friday."

"That's silly," he said sharply, acknowledging more disappointment than he ought to be feeling. There was an unaccustomed tightness in his chest. "I want you there as soon as possible. Why wait until Friday?"

"Because my mother would expect it," she said heatedly.

"Your mother would—oh." Belatedly he realized what she meant. He almost laughed aloud, to think that someone would still be so concerned with observing the proprieties. Then he saw that she was dead serious. He sighed in frustration, bringing one hand up to roughly massage his chest. "All right. But I still think it's silly." *Especially given the fact that nothing will be changing after you do move in.*

"Fortunately," she said in a honeyed tone, "I don't particularly care what you think."

"Yes, you've already made that plain," he said, recalling the way he'd found out she quit school after the fact.

Then she homed in on the rest of his original statement. "What things do we have to do?"

"Wedding dress," he said briefly, glancing at her

again to gauge her reaction. "And wedding plans."
Faith wasn't quite as pliable as her quiet nature suggested, a fact he seemed to be learning the hard way.

Her eyes went wide and then her fair elegant
brows drew together. "Absolutely not. I'm not wearing a real wedding dress. I have an ivory silk suit,
fairly dressy, that ought to do."

"I have a woman meeting us at the house at one
with a large selection." He took a deep breath, fighting the urge to bark out orders. Faith wasn't one of
his employees and if he shouted at her, she was liable
to bolt. "If you don't want a big, fluffy wedding
dress, that's fine. But our mothers—not to mention
the press—are going to expect you to look something
like a bride."

"It's really none of the press's business."

"I know. But when you have as much money as
I do, you wield a certain amount of influence. And
influence leads to attention, even though I don't seek
it out." A quick glance at her expression told him
she hadn't bought it yet. "Like it or not, we're going
to be of interest to the public. Think of yourself
as...sort of a princess of a minor kingdom. Royalty
interests everyone. And since there's no royalty in
America, the wealthy get pestered."

She sighed. "It's that important to you?"

He hesitated. There was an odd note in her voice,
though he couldn't decipher it. "Yes," he said finally. "It's that important to me. This has to look
real. If anyone should suspect it isn't..." He looked
over at her while he waited at a light, but she had
linked her hands in her lap and was studying them.
He was sure she was going to object again, or perhaps even refuse to marry him. He took a deep

breath, deliberately expanding his lungs to full capacity, but still he had that taut, binding sensation gripping him.

Then she said, "All right. I'll come to your home and see these dresses."

His whole body relaxed and the air whooshed from his lungs with an audible sound.

She shot a questioning glance at him. He'd better get a grip. She was going to think this meant more to him than it did. All he wanted, he reminded himself, was to inherit the company that had been his mother's family's. He'd known before he'd ever embarked on this course of action that this was to be a marriage with a finite limit of time. And in any case, he had no business even thinking about Faith in any terms other than those of a...a what? A guardian and his ward was definitely too archaic. A sister? No, there was no way he could ever condition himself to think of her as a sister. A friend? There. They could be friends. That was by far the most suitable description of their relationship, both now and in the future.

Inside him, though, there was a little voice laughing uproariously. *A friend? Does kissing a friend get you so hot and bothered you barely remember your own mother is in the room?*

Shut up, he told the voice. Just—shut—up.

But all he said aloud to Faith was "That's great. Thank you."

Friday morning finally arrived. Standing in the courthouse with his mother, he checked his watch. Almost time. Where the hell was Faith? He knew he should have made her move in before this. Then he could have kept an eye on her, made sure she didn't get cold feet.

It had been a surprisingly long week. He'd caught himself glancing at his watch throughout meetings and conference calls practically every hour since he'd dropped Faith off at her apartment to pack on Monday after her private showing of wedding dresses.

Which she hadn't let him see.

He frowned. Whoever would have suspected the stubborn streak hiding behind that angelic face? It would be bad luck, she'd told him.

Just then, an older woman walked around the corner. Spying him, her face lit up and she hurried forward. "Hello, Mr. Lachlan. We're here."

It was...what was her name? Clarice. Faith's mother's...friend. Caregiver. Whatever.

"Hello, Clarice," he said. "Have you seen Faith?"

"Oh, she's here. We all came together." Clarice extended a hand to his mother. "Hello. I'm Clarice Nealy, Faith's mother's companion."

He felt a dull embarrassment at his lapse of manners. "Oh, sorry. Clarice, this is my mother, Eliza Smythe." The two women shook hands.

His mother only smiled at him. "We forgive you." To Clarice, she said, "He's going to have a stroke if he doesn't get to see his bride soon."

Stone ignored that and consulted his watch. "It's our turn. What is she doing?" Impatiently he strode toward the corner, but Clarice's voice stopped him.

"No, no. You go in. Faith and her mother will be here in a moment."

He frowned, but when his mother took his arm, he sighed and led her into the room.

The justice of the peace stood at the front of the room in front of a wooden rail. To one side of him was a massive raised bench behind which the man presided over his courtroom, with state and national flags displayed behind it. He looked a little startled as Stone and his mother walked forward. "Hello. You are Stone Lachlan and Faith Harrell?"

Eliza Smythe started to chuckle. "No. The bride isn't here yet."

Just then, the door to the small chamber opened and he caught a glimpse of Clarice's beaming face as she held it wide. Faith's mother, seated on a motorized scooter, whirred into the room and stopped just inside the door. Then Faith stepped into the doorway and reached for her mother's hand.

The whole room seemed to freeze for one long moment as he simply stared. His heart leaped, then settled down to a fast thudding in his chest.

She looked stunning. As she walked toward him, pacing herself to the speed of her mother's scooter at her side, he had to remind himself to breathe.

She had chosen a short dress rather than anything long and formal. An underlayer was made of some shiny satiny fabric that fit her like a second skin, showcasing her slender figure. The satin, covered by a thin, lacy overlayer, was strapless and low-cut and against his will his eyes were drawn to the shadowed swell of creamy flesh revealed above its edge. Over the satin, the sheath of fine sheer lace covered her up to the neck, though it clearly wasn't designed to hide anything, but rather to enhance. This layer had long close-fitting sleeves and extended in a lacy scallop just below the hem of the underdress.

He took in the rest of her. Her hair was up in a smooth, gleaming fancy twist of some kind and she wore flowers in it, arranged around a crown of shining gems. As he recalled his reference to royalty, he had to suppress a grin. She'd done that deliberately, the little tease. She carried the small but exquisite trailing bouquet of palest peach roses, Peruvian lilies and white dendrobium orchids with touches of feathery greens that he'd sent to her. The subtle touch of color was the perfect enhancement for the glowing white of the dress.

It didn't escape his notice that she'd chosen pure, virginal white for her wedding day. Probably a good thing, since it served to remind him of the liaison they had—and its limits.

Limits. God, what he wouldn't give to be able to show her the pleasures of lovemaking. For an instant, he allowed himself to imagine that this was real, that the beautiful, desirable woman coming toward him would be his wife in every way. If this was real, it would be just the beginning. He would enjoy the incredible pleasures her soft body promised, and come home to her warm arms every night. In due course they would add children to their family—

Whoa! *Children?* He gave himself a firm mental kick in the butt.

Faith had reached his side by now and he surveyed her face as she turned to kiss her mother and then his. She wore more makeup than usual and the normal beauty of her features now approached a porcelain perfection. Her skin seemed lit by an inner radiance. She'd curled small wisps of her hair and it gently bounced around her face in soft, shining waves that made him want to sink his fingers into it simply to experience the texture. But he couldn't do that. He couldn't touch her in any but the most innocuous of ways.

The justice cleared his throat and Stone realized the ceremony was about to begin. His mother flanked him and Naomi maneuvered her scooter to Faith's far side. Clarice took a seat in the small rows of chairs behind them. He extended his arm to Faith and she took it, smiling up at him tentatively.

He didn't smile back. The reminder that this was a forced union of sorts had ruined the moment for him. This was a ridiculous charade, necessitated by the intransigence of his mother. It was, at best, an inconvenience, an interruption, in his life as well as Faith's. There was nothing to smile about.

The smile faded from her face when he didn't respond and she dropped her gaze. Her face abruptly assumed the serene contours he knew meant she was hiding her thoughts from the world, and she turned toward the official who was beginning the ceremony.

Too late to catch her eye, he regretted his action. Now he felt like a real bastard. She'd clearly wanted a little reassurance. He glanced down at her fine profile as she stood beside him, one small hand resting in the crook of his arm. To his dismay, he realized she was blinking rapidly, her silver eyes misted with a sheen of tears. Damn!

Acting on instinct, he raised his free hand and covered hers on his opposite arm, squeezing gently.

She looked up at him again and offered him a wobbly smile. Remorse shot through him. She was only twenty years old. He doubted this was what she'd envisioned when she'd dreamed of her wedding day, even though she'd insisted on this extreme simplicity when they'd discussed it.

He smiled down at her as he passed an arm behind her back and gave her shoulders a gentle hug. She felt small and soft beneath his hand, and he liked the way her slender curves pressed against his side far too well. Tough. He wasn't going to do anything about *that* but he could make this day less of a chore for each of them.

The ceremony was short and impersonal as the justice of the peace sealed the bonds of matrimony with swift efficiency. Faith spoke her responses in a quiet, steady tone, looking down at their hands as they exchanged rings and in a shockingly brief matter of minutes, they were legally bound.

The justice looked incredibly bored; how many of these things did he perform in a week's time? "You may kiss your bride," the man intoned.

Stone set his hands at Faith's waist and drew her toward him. As his mouth descended, she raised her face to his and his lips slid onto hers. He froze for an instant, nearly seduced by the sweet, soft flesh of her full lips and the memory of the way she'd melted in his arms on Sunday night. But this couldn't be. It *couldn't be,* he told himself fiercely. Faith wasn't experienced enough to know that sex and love were two distinct issues in a man's mind. He would be courting a messy, emotional disaster if he couldn't keep his distance from her. And so, steeling himself to the powerful allure of her person, he kept the kiss brief and impersonal, then drew back.

He felt her go rigid beneath his hands, and he nearly apologized, but as the words formed, he realized how strange *that* would sound to the witnesses, so he swallowed the apology and settled instead for, "Are you ready to go?"

Faith nodded. She wouldn't look at him and he gritted his teeth against the urge to raise her chin and cover her lips with his own again.

Oh, hell. No, no, and *no!* He wasn't going to do anything stupid with Randall Harrell's daughter. His ward. This marriage was just a business arrangement, of a sort.

Of course it was.

Faith woke early on her first morning as a married woman. For a moment, she didn't recognize her surroundings and then it all came flooding back. Yesterday she had married Stone.

Married. She raised her left hand and her new rings sparkled as the faceted stones caught the light. If it weren't for these she'd think it had been a dream. Slowly she got to her feet and headed for the bathroom. As she showered and dressed, she couldn't keep herself from reviewing the wedding ceremony, like a child who couldn't resist picking at a healing wound.

Stone had looked so handsome in the severe cut of the morning suit he'd worn. As she'd come into the courtroom, she'd allowed herself to fantasize, for one brief instant, that she was a real bride, flushed and brimming with love for her husband, taking his name and becoming part of his life forever. But then she'd looked into Stone's eyes and seen nothing. Nothing. No feeling, no warmth. No love. He'd quickly tried to cover it up, but that first impression was indelibly stamped on her mind.

She felt her bottom lip tremble and she bit down on it fiercely. For the first time, she allowed herself to acknowledge the depths of her disappointment. She hadn't married Stone entirely because of their bargain. She'd married him because somewhere in the past week her silly, girlish crush had gelled into a deeper, more mature emotion.

Oh, it hurt even to think it and she shied away from deeper examination of her feelings.

Instead she replayed the wedding scene in her mind again. And she realized her shattered heart had forgotten something. He did have *some* feelings for her. Recalling the look in his eye the first night he'd kissed her, she knew with a deep inner feeling of feminine certainty that he wanted her, at least in the physical sense. And yesterday, for the briefest instant before his gaze had grown cool and distant, she'd seen the poleaxed look on his face as he absorbed the sight of her in her wedding dress. And she'd been gratified, because she'd chosen the unconventional wedding dress, her makeup and the soft, pretty hairstyle for the express purpose of making him notice her.

Yes, for that one unguarded moment, there had been no doubt that he wanted her. If she was going to remember the cold shoulder, she needed to cling to this memory, too. And though she knew it was foolish to believe she could parlay that basic sexual desire into a more lasting emotion, that was exactly what she hoped.

He wanted her. It was a start. And she…she wanted him as well. Wanted him to be the one to teach her the intimacies of the sexual act, wanted him to make love to her. Maybe she could attract his feelings the same way her body attracted his.

Perhaps they would begin to communicate better when they went on their honeymoon. Though she knew Stone hadn't planned one, he'd told his mother they would be going away a few weeks from now. He'd only said it because Eliza had very pointedly asked where he intended to take Faith, she was certain. And she knew he would follow through if only to assuage any doubt in his mother's mind about the veracity of their marriage.

Buoyed by the thought, she made her bed and headed downstairs. The newspaper was lying on the kitchen counter and there was fresh coffee, signs that Stone must already be up. She hunted through the cupboards until she found cereal and dishes, and ate while she leafed through the paper. But all her nerve endings were quivering, alert, waiting for him to enter the room.

When she heard him coming down the hall, she quickly ducked her head behind the paper again, looking up innocently as he entered. "Good morning."

"Good morning. Did you sleep well?" He barely glanced at her as he headed for the coffeepot and poured himself a cup.

"Quite, thank you. And you?"

"Fine." He sounded grumpy. Maybe he wasn't a morning person, though he certainly looked like he was awake and alert. Lord, it simply wasn't fair for the man to look so absolutely stunning first thing in the morning. He was as handsome to her as always and her heart rate increased as a wave of tenderness swept through her. She was his *wife!* Then she realized he was saying something else.

"Your mother and Clarice will be moving in today. I have a company bringing her household up late this morning. Will you help her arrange everything when it arrives?"

"Of course." It shouldn't bother her that he hadn't asked her opinion. Although she'd have preferred to go down and help Clarice pack, she knew this way would be much faster and more efficient.

Stone seemed unaware of her thoughts. "I know it's Saturday but I have to go in to my office for a few hours, so I'll leave that to you." He opened the door of the refrigerator and she saw a large casserole dish. "That's a chicken and broccoli casserole the housekeeper made and froze. I set it in there to thaw. If you want to invite your mother and Clarice to eat with us tonight, that's fine with me."

She nodded. "Is there anything else you'd like me to do? Until the summer sessions begin, I'm going to have a ton of time on my hands. I have some accounting skills and I know my way around a computer. Maybe I could help in your office—"

But he was chuckling. "I employ people to do all that," he said. "Just consider the next two months a vacation."

Disappointment rushed through her for more than one reason. She hated to be idle. And working for him would give them something in common. "Oh, but I could use the experience—"

"Tell you what," he said, cutting her off again. "I know something you could do that would help immensely."

Thrilled, she sat up straighter. "What?"

"The den," he said.

The den? *What* in the den?

"I've never had it redecorated," he continued. "It's something I've thought about a lot and just never gotten around to doing. But it needs a facelift desperately. The easy chair my father sat in for years is still in there." Now he looked at her hopefully. "Would you consider taking on that project?"

"Of course," she said. "Just tell me what color scheme you like. But also, I—"

"I trust your judgment," he said. "Anything fairly neutral." He headed for the door, coffee cup in hand. "I've got to get going. I have an early meeting this morning. Enjoy your day."

"Oh, yeah, it ought to be a blast," she muttered as she heard the front door close. Redecorate the den. Was he serious? She'd intended to help him at the office. She didn't care if she was a receptionist. It would certainly be better experience than redecorating the stupid den! She should have told him how insulting she'd found that...giving her a little wifely project to do when what she really wanted was to be working for him, in whatever capacity he could use her.

Yikes. Her mind took that last thought and gave it a distinctly sexual twist as the memory of his hard, hot body pressed against her side while they spoke their vows set her heart racing again. She still was trying to get used to the perpetual breathless state that being around Stone left her in since the night he'd kissed her in front of his mother and turned her world upside down.

He'd kissed her when they'd gotten married, too, and though that had been only the merest correct meeting of lips, she was sure it had short-circuited some of her brain cells. It certainly had sealed her fate. And with that thought, she forced herself to face the truth.

She hadn't married Stone Lachlan because he needed her help. And she hadn't married him because it was a way to pay him back for his financial support, or because he'd promised to take care of her mother, or because he had promised to help her finish school. No, she'd married him because she was in love with him.

She took a deep breath. *Okay, you've admitted it.* She'd loved him, she supposed, for years under the guise of having a crush. Only the crush had deepened more and more as she'd come to know him, as she'd seen what a decent, honorable man he was, what a thoughtful, caring person—and how incredibly potent his appeal was.

And that was her misfortune. He'd made it abundantly clear, over and over again, that this was a business arrangement, not one in which emotion was welcome.

Well, tough. He might consider it business, but she was declaring war. She had a year. Three hundred and sixty-five days. Surely within that time she could make herself such an integral part of his life that he'd wake up one day and realize he loved her, too.

Having Faith's mother and Clarice around the house wasn't the burden he'd expected it to be, Stone thought a week later as he sat at the kitchen counter nursing a cup of coffee. In fact, it was a distinct blessing.

He'd encouraged the older women to join them for

dinner each night. And though they'd both protested at first, he'd made it his goal to charm them. And he'd succeeded. He hadn't had to spend more than a few moments alone with Faith all week. Yes, inviting her mother here had been a great idea.

It might be the only thing that kept him from grabbing his young bride and ravishing her for the remaining fifty-one weeks of what was shaping up to be one damned long year.

He heaved a sigh, propping his elbows on the counter and pressing the heels of his palms against his temples. God, but Faith was making it difficult to be noble! He had no intention of seducing her. It would be despicable of him to use her that way for the brief term of their marriage and then discard her when they split up, as they intended to do.

And maybe if he kept telling himself that long enough, he'd believe it. He could hear her first thing in the morning, moving around in her bathroom, humming in the shower, removing hangers from her closet and replacing them. His active imagination supplied visual details in Technicolor. She joined him over breakfast, no matter how early he got up, and her soft farewell was the last thing he heard before he left. In the evening, she always came to greet him at the door with a smile, taking his coat and preparing dinner while he changed into casual clothes. It was a treat not to have to eat alone all the time.

And then there was her relationship with her mother. Faith and Naomi were closer than they had any right to be, considering how little they'd really seen of each other during Faith's adolescent years. They teased and smiled, shared stories about Faith's father, worked crossword puzzles together, and genuinely seemed to treasure each moment spent together. It was such a marked contrast to his relationship with his own mother that he could get jealous if he let himself think about it long enough. Sure, he'd imagined that normal families had relationships like that, but until he'd seen exactly how close and loving Faith and her mother were, it had been an abstract concept. Now, thanks to them, it was a reality.

He could hear them laughing right now as they came in from an early walk—or drive, in Naomi's case—through Central Park, across the street from the town house. In a moment, they were in the kitchen.

"We're back." Faith greeted him with a smile as she helped her mother out of her coat and took it to hang in the closet. "It's a beautiful day. Spring is definitely on the way."

"The prediction is for snow by the first of the week," he warned her.

"But it won't last," she said confidently.

Naomi directed her motorized scooter toward her own apartment down the hall from the kitchen and the two of them were left alone. An awkward moment of silence passed.

Then Faith cleared her throat. "Do you have anything planned for today?"

"Um, nothing special," he said. "Tonight there's a dinner and ball but we have most of the day before we have to start getting ready for that."

"That reminds me," she said, snapping her fingers. "Is there anything in particular you'd like me to wear to the ball? I have those dresses we bought last week, remember?''

He remembered. And his blood heated. Though she hadn't modeled them for him, he'd had several long, detailed daydreams. "How about the blue?" he said.

"All right." She cleared her throat. "Actually, if you have time, I'd like you to look at some fabric swatches and paint colors for the den. I can order things next week."

He didn't really want to spend any more time alone with her than he absolutely had to, but she vanished before he could think of a good reason not to look at the samples. A few moments later she reappeared clutching a large folder and two wallpaper books. He folded up his paper and efficiently, she spread everything out on the counter. Her slim figure, clad in blue jeans and a clinging pale yellow sweater, was so close he could smell the clean scent of her hair, and her shoulder brushed against his side as she moved. "Here you go." She pulled one of the wallpaper books toward them. "The first thing you need to do is decide on the walls. Then we'll go from there."

"You're really happy to have your mother here, aren't you?" Good God. Why had he said that?

Her fingers stilled on the books. "Yes. Thank you again."

"No," he said impatiently. Hell, he'd started this, he might as well find out what he really wanted to know. "I mean, you're enjoying her company, not just putting on a polite act."

Her eyebrows rose. "Why on earth would I do that? Of course I'm enjoying her company. No, I take that back. I'm *loving* it. At school, there were nights when I cried myself to sleep, missing her so much. It wasn't that the school was a terrible place,'' she said hastily as he frowned. "The staff members were actually very caring and mostly I was happy. And I could call Mama every day if I liked. But it still wasn't the same.''

"No, I guess it wasn't.'' He could hear the longing in her voice as she relived those days and he felt a surprising kinship. "But you understood how difficult it would have been for her to try to care for you at home. You knew she would have done it if she could.''

She turned and looked at him, her gray eyes far too wise and understanding. "I think your mother cares, too. Maybe it wasn't as easy for her to leave you as you think.''

"I don't think about it,'' he said. He didn't want her pitying him, thinking he'd had a miserable childhood. "My father and I got along fine without her.''

She didn't say a word, only studied him.

"She could have pretended she cared,'' he said, goaded by her silence. "Would it have killed her to let a little kid think he meant something special to her?''

Faith laid her small hand on his arm and he realized how tense he was. "I don't know,'' she said. "Have you ever asked her?''

He consciously relaxed his muscles, feeling the tension drain out of him. "No.'' He reached forward and pulled the wallpaper books toward him. This conversation was pointless. "It doesn't matter anymore. Now why don't you show me what you have in mind?''

She continued to gaze at him for a long moment, and he kept his eyes on the books. He didn't want her pity. Sure, he'd been hurt by his mother's indifference when he was small, but he was a grown man now, and her approval had long ceased to matter to him.

"All right," she finally said. She rested one hand on the back of his chair and opened the topmost book with the other. The action placed her breasts just below eye level, inches away, and he couldn't prevent himself from covertly assessing the rounded mounds. "Here you go. The first thing to decide on is—"

"Look." He pushed back his chair and rose before he gave in to the fantasy that had leaped into his head. "I want you to like the den, too," he said. "I don't need to approve it. I'm sure whatever you choose will be fine."

"You're the one who's going to have to live with it after I leave," she pointed out.

After I leave… The words echoed in the air around them and he was shocked by the strong urge to blurt out "Don't leave!"

But he didn't say it. Instead images of his life a year from now, when Faith and her family were gone and he was rattling around this place alone again, bombarded him. He *liked* having Naomi and Clarice around, dammit! And he more than liked having Faith around. For one brief instant he allowed himself to imagine what it would be like to grow old with her, to stay married to her on a permanent basis. The thought was so tantalizingly appealing that he immediately shoved it away.

Abruptly he turned his back and started out of the room. "I don't have time to deal with this now."

Five

That evening, Faith showered and shampooed, then rubbed silky cream into her skin and rolled her hair in large hot rollers that left it frothy and bouncy around her shoulders. It would be a lie, she thought as she applied a heavier-than-normal makeup suitable for evening, if she didn't feel the slightest bit pleased by his reaction to her in the morning. When she'd stood close to Stone at the breakfast bar, he definitely had been uncomfortable. And she was pretty sure it wasn't because he was worried about her decorating skills. She'd noticed him looking at her body out of the corner of his eye. And before that, he'd talked about his mother.

Okay, those few sentences weren't much to go on, but she couldn't expect him to be too voluble at first. That would come later, after they'd gotten closer, she hoped. She slipped into a strapless bra and panties

and donned the pretty Escada with the silver trim that
Stone had asked her to wear. The Prada heels and a
small silver clutch bag completed the ensemble and
as she glanced into the full-length mirror in the bathroom, a small thrill ran through her.

She'd never owned anything so beautiful before.
Thanks to the snug bodice of the strapless dress and
the bra beneath it, she had genuinely respectable
cleavage. The silver and blue layers of the full skirt
swayed as she left her room and walked down the
stairs to meet Stone.

He was standing in the archway to the formal front
room with his back to her as she rounded the turn
on the landing and continued down toward him, one
hand lightly trailing on the banister as a precaution,
since she wasn't used to such high heels. When he
heard her footsteps he turned—

And for one long, strangely intense moment, the
air seemed to shimmer between them. His gaze
started at her toes and swept up her body, leaving
her quivering in reaction and her steps slowed and
stopped as his eyes bored into hers. She simply
stood, halfway down the steps, held immobile by that
gaze and she felt her breath quicken as a heavy, unfamiliar pressure coiled low in her abdomen.

Finally Stone cleared his throat. "I'll be the envy
of every man in the room."

The spell was broken but she was warmed by his
words. "That would be nice," she said, finishing her
descent and stopping in front of him. "I'll try to be
an asset to you."

Stone smiled but it looked a little strained and she
realized the barrier he'd put between them earlier in
the day was still firmly in place. Then he smiled.

"The first time I ever met you, you had a ponytail so long you could sit on the end of it. It's a little disconcerting to see you looking so grown-up and gorgeous."

"Thank you. I think." She wasn't particularly pleased with the hint that he still thought of her as a child, and she knew he'd done it deliberately. But she didn't comment. "You look very nice, too. I've never seen you in a tux before."

"A necessary evil." He dropped her hand and turned away, picking up a small box from an etagere beneath a large gilt-framed mirror. "I have a wedding gift for you."

She was dismayed. "But...I didn't get anything for you."

"Agreeing to this charade was gift enough." He lifted her limp hand from her side and pressed the velvet case into it. "Open it."

Automatically she lifted the other hand to support the box, which was heavier than she'd expected. "Stone, I—"

"Open it," he said again, impatience ripe in his tone. "Don't forget you're Mrs. Stone Lachlan now. People would talk if I didn't have you dripping with gems."

Slowly she nodded, then bent her head and pried open the hinged box. And gasped.

Nestled on black velvet was a necklace of brilliant blue sapphires and diamonds. The alternating colored stones glinted gaily in the light from the crystal chandelier overhead, smaller stones back near the ornate platinum clasp gently graduating in size to a significant sapphire anchor in the middle. Matching teardrop earrings were fastened to the velvet as well.

She was speechless. Literally. Her mouth was as dry as a bone. There was nothing she could do but stare at the striking jewelry, not even blinking. Never, in her entire life, had she seen stones like these up close and personal. Unless you counted the glass display behind which the Hope Diamond rested at the Smithsonian in Washington.

Stone took the box from her and removed the necklace. "Turn around."

Obediently she turned around, and in a moment she felt the cool weight of the platinum and gems against her skin as Stone's fingers grazed her nape. This felt like a dream. Just weeks ago, she'd been waiting on customers at Saks; today she was married to one of the wealthiest men in the country and he was showering her with clothing and jewels. A few months ago, she'd been a college student with no idea that every penny of her education was being paid for out of the goodness of someone's heart.

Flustered and agitated, she whipped around to face Stone. "I can't do this."

"Do what?" He raised his hands and clasped her upper arms gently, rubbing his thumbs back and forth over the sensitive flesh.

She shivered as goose bumps popped up all over her body and a quick *zing* of mouth-drying, breath-shortening attraction shot through her. She was so close she could see the flecks of amber and gold amid the blue in his irises when she looked up and abruptly she realized her change of position had placed them in a decidedly intimate pose. Her breasts grazed the solid expanse of tuxedo-clad chest and the way in which he held her made her feel strangely small and delicate.

"You know." She stepped back a pace and raised her hands to try to unclasp the necklace. "Pretend to be your wife—"

"There's nothing pretend about it, Faith," he said. "You *are* my wife."

"Not in every way," she said steadily though she knew she was blushing and her whole body felt trembly and weak.

His hands dropped away from her as if her skin burned his flesh. "No," he said. "That was our agreement."

"We could…change the terms, if we wanted to." She didn't know where she'd found the courage to speak to him so frankly, but she was conscious of every hour of her year sliding by.

But he was shaking his head. "No. It's normal for us to be attracted to each other in a situation like this. But acting on it would be a huge mistake." He took the box from her and removed the earrings, then handed them to her as matter-of-factly as if they hadn't just had the most intimate conversation of their acquaintance. "Put these on and then we'll go."

She wanted to say more but she didn't have the courage. He'd turned her down flat, crushing her hopes. Numbly she fastened the earrings through her ears and picked up her small purse again.

"Aren't you even going to look at them?" Stone took her shoulders and angled her to look in the mirror over the table. Reflected back was an elegant, beautiful woman wearing a stunning sapphire-and-diamond collar and matching earrings. Behind her, his hands possessively cupping her shoulders, was a tall, handsome man in a tuxedo, confidence oozing from every pore.

A perfect match. She turned away from the mirror, fighting tears. They looked so right together, confirming her feelings. How could he think making love would be a mistake?

"What is this fund-raiser for?" Faith asked as they stepped into the grand ballroom a little while later.

Stone grinned, feeling a spark of genuine amusement as he anticipated her response. "It's not quite the typical political occasion," he said. "It's for WARR."

"War?" Her eyebrows rose.

"Wild Animal Rescue and Rehabilitation. The organization rescues lions, cheetahs, tigers, elephants, bears…you name it, from bad situations. They restore them to health and place them in zoos, parks and other habitats where they'll be able to live in peace."

She nodded, her eyes lighting up. "That's wonderful. I read an article about Tippi Hedren's efforts with the great cats recently. It's horrifying to hear some of the stories about the way those poor animals are forced to live."

"It's also horrifying that people think they'll make great pets." He took her hand and directed her toward a large display near the entrance, where guests were perusing photos and stories about WARR's work. "A child in Wyoming recently was killed by a tiger that her neighbor owned as a pet—uh-oh." Catching sight of the woman bearing down on them, he squeezed her hand once in warning. "Brace yourself. We're about to face the inquisition."

"Stone Lachlan!" It was a woman's voice, booming and imperious. "Where have you been hiding yourself?"

Stone kissed the rouged cheek of the tiny woman who approached. "Mrs. deLatoure. What a pleasure. I've been working rather than hiding, but I'm glad I took a break tonight. Otherwise, I might have missed seeing you."

The little woman beamed. "Outrageous flattery. Feel free to continue."

Eunicia deLatoure was the widowed matriarch of one of the country's wealthiest, oldest wine-making families. Her sons had taken over the business a few years ago when her husband had passed away but the widow deLatoure was still a force to be reckoned with. Rumor had it that her sons ran every major decision by her before plunging into anything. Having met her quiet, deferential sons before, Stone didn't doubt it.

He slipped an arm around Faith's waist then and drew her forward, enjoying the feel of her slender body in his grasp as he made a perfunctory introduction. This night was going to be both heaven and hell. Especially now that he knew what she was thinking. Did she have any idea what she was asking for? He seriously doubted it. He was pretty sure she was still a virgin. Damn, *that* was the wrong thing to think about!

"Your bride! I just read about your engagement a few days ago." The woman's eyes flew wide and the stentorian tones turned heads throughout a solid quadrant of the ballroom. She leveled a piercing gaze on Faith. "Congratulations, my dear. I assume this is a recent development."

"Very recent. We're still in the honeymoon stage."

Stone answered before Faith could open her mouth.
"And we're feeling quite smug to have kept it a
secret from the press."

The matriarch chuckled. Then her gaze sharpened
as she pinned Faith with that gimlet eye again. "It's
delightful to meet you. Is your family in attendance
tonight?"

It was a blatant attempt to ferret out Faith's ped-
igree, he knew. "No." He answered before she could
speak. "Just me." He pulled her closer to his side.
"It's good to see you, Mrs. D. Say hello to Luc and
Henri for me."

As he steered Faith away, she said, "I could have
spoken for myself, you know. The woman probably
thinks you married a mute."

He registered the slightly testy tone in her voice.
"Sorry. I just didn't want her to grill you. She can
be merciless." As he continued across the room, he
muttered in her ear, "We don't have to worry about
spreading the news anymore. I bet every person in
this ballroom knows we're married within ten
minutes."

"That's what you wanted, isn't it?" Her gaze was
steady and there were unspoken issues dancing between them.

"Yeah," he said, ignoring everything but the
words. "That's what I wanted." Purposefully he
moved through the crowd enjoying drinks and can-
apés, introducing Faith as they went.

The band switched from background music to
dance tunes and the floor filled immediately. When
he heard the strains of the first slow dance, he took
her glass and his and set them both aside. "Do you

like to dance?'' he asked as he escorted her to the floor.

"I don't really know," she said. "I've never done much of it."

"You're kidding. What did they teach you at that school?"

"Latin, physics, biology…little things like that. It was a *real* school."

"Point taken," he said, amused. "All right, I'll teach you to dance. Just step where I step and hold on to me."

"How about I just stand on your feet like I used to?"

He laughed. "Let's see how you do learning the steps before we resort to that."

When they reached the dance floor, he pulled her into the rhythm of the steps with ease, guiding her with one big hand on her back. His fingers grazed her skin just above the place where her dress stopped. God, he wanted to touch her in so many other ways. This was torture. But it was necessary. They had to appear to be a happy newly married couple. The first few weeks were bound to be the toughest, until their marriage faded from the radar screens of the gossip-mongers.

"Are you doing all right?" he asked. She was following his lead easily, as if they had danced together a hundred times before.

She nodded, the action stirring the soft curls against her neck. "Fine."

"Good." He hesitated, then said, "I'm going to hold you closer. The world is watching and I want them to be convinced we're newlyweds." *Uh-huh, ri-i-ight,* said his conscience, but he firmly squashed it.

"All right." Her voice was breathy, her color high. Her gaze flashed to his, then away, and the desire she felt was so transparent he felt scorched by the heat that leaped between them.

Dammit, this was impossible. Knowing that she wanted him was the worst kind of aphrodisiac in the world. If she were more experienced, he wouldn't hesitate to take what she offered. But she wasn't. And he had no intention of changing their situation. Someday she would thank him for it. He hoped so, anyhow, because if she didn't appreciate how hard this was for him, he might just strangle her.

How hard...bad choice of words. Very bad choice of words. He drew her in, tucking their clasped hands to his chest and sliding his arm more fully around her, bringing her body closer to his without pressing her torso against his. Thank God she was wearing that puffy-skirted dress that made it hard, er, *difficult* for him to get too close. She'd probably be shocked silly if she realized exactly what she was pressed against, because for all her delicate dancing around a very touchy subject, he knew her experience was extremely limited. The first time he'd kissed her he'd sensed that she hadn't had a lot of practice at it. But she'd learned fast. Thinking about her passionate, searing response to his kiss was a bad idea. A really, really lousy idea, in fact. He tried to concentrate on the music, the couples around them, but all he could seem to absorb was the feel of her in his arms. She startled him then by turning her face into his throat, tilting it slightly upward so that her breath caressed his throat and resting her head against his shoulder and without thinking, he slid his hand up over the bare skin of her back to caress her nape.

She shivered involuntarily, and he smiled against her hair. "Sorry. Did I tickle you?"

"N-no."

"Good. Relax." *Was she kissing his neck?* No, of course she wasn't. It was only his prurient imagination in overdrive. "People are watching us. You do realize we're going to be the hot topic of tomorrow's gossip column, don't you?"

"I hope not." Her breath lightly feathered his skin.

"We are. But as I said, they'll soon be on to some newer gossip. We'll be so boring they won't have anything to write about."

"Good." Her answer was heartfelt.

They danced in silence for a long while as the music flowed from one song into another. He thought he probably could hold her, just like this, all night. Their silence wasn't strained, and though his body was well aware of her nearness, there was a strangely satisfying peaceful sweetness in simply dancing with her in his arms. The thought of doing this week after week for an entire year was powerfully appealing. His blood fizzed and bubbled like fine sparkling wine in his veins and reluctantly, he acknowledged that he was going to have to put some space between them or he was going to do something he would definitely regret.

"Faith?"

"Hmm?"

"When this song ends, we're leaving."

She raised her head from his shoulder and immediately he missed the warmth. "It's barely ten o'clock. Isn't that a bit early?"

"Not for newlyweds. They'll think they know exactly where we're going."

"Oh." Her eyes widened and her gaze clung to his for a long moment. Then she dropped the contact and looked steadily at his right shoulder, which he knew was all she could see from her angle. She'd withdrawn from him, he realized. And a second later, he also realized he didn't like it one damn bit.

"Faith?"

"Yes?" She didn't look at him.

The hell with distance. He had to taste her again or die. "I'm going to kiss you."

"Wha—?" Her eyes flew open and she instinctively tried to pull away from him, but he controlled her with such ease that he doubted anyone even realized she'd just lost a bid for freedom. "Why?" she asked bluntly. "You said I—you said you didn't want me—"

"Appearances." His voice sounded strained to his own ears. "I'm going to kiss you so there's no doubt in anyone's mind why we're leaving." *Liar.*

"Oh." It took the wind out of her sails and he almost could feel her droop against him. She was so vulnerable that one short comment had wounded her. It was a puzzle. How could a woman as lovely as Faith think she wasn't attractive? Then he realized that she'd simply never been exposed to large quantities of men who would undoubtedly drool over her. He sighed, unable to let her continue thinking that she didn't turn him on.

"It's not you," he said gruffly. "You're the most desirable woman I've ever known and if you want the truth, I'm having a hell of a time keeping myself from, uh, doing something rash.''

There was a silence between them.

Finally she said, "Really?" and her tone was distinctly doubtful.

"Really," he responded dryly.

"It, um, wouldn't be rash," she said, looking up at him with such hope in her eyes that he felt ten feet tall.

His body urged him to take her somewhere private and plunge into the maelstrom of passion she offered—but he resisted. He still wasn't going to make any moves they both would regret later. He had to kiss her, but he would keep it short. Just a taste to get him through this ridiculously adolescent longing. "Selfish, then. Your whole life is ahead of you. You need time to experience the world."

She didn't say anything, just lowered her gaze to his shoulder again, giving him a subtle but definite cold shoulder.

Now he knew exactly what his married buddies called "the silent treatment." And he knew why they didn't like it. Well, the hell with that. Letting go of the hand he held in closed dance position, he took her stubborn little chin in his fingers and tipped her face up to his. And then his lips slid onto hers and the world exploded.

He initially had intended to give her a light, gentle kiss that would look romantic to the many eyes covertly directed their way. But the minute he began to kiss her, Faith relaxed against him with a quiet hum of approval, delighting him and pushing his already eager body into a far-too-serious awareness of the girl who was, in the strictest sense of the word, his ward until her twenty-first birthday. God, she was so innocent! He could taste the inexperience in the sweet soft line of her lips as she passively let him mold them, and he moved carefully, determined not to scare her.

But she didn't seem to be in any danger of being frightened. He suppressed a groan as her lips began to move beneath his. Slowly he lifted his mouth a breath away from hers, knowing he couldn't take much more. They were on a dance floor in the middle of a crowded ballroom; even if he intended to deepen the kiss and teach her how to kiss him back the way he longed for her to do, he wasn't going to do it here.

You aren't going to do it ever.

Ever. He looked down at her, taking in the glaze of passion in her eyes and the way she ran her tongue over her lips in reaction as she said, "Stone?" in a bewildered tone.

"That should convince them." He forced out the words, ignoring her unspoken appeal. "Thanks."

Her eyes widened and her body went stiff in his arms. Carefully she pushed herself away from the close contact and let him continue to lead her through the motions of the dance. But she'd lowered her head and withdrawn into herself again. He could feel the distance between them and abruptly, he led her off the dance floor.

No matter how much he wanted to pull her back against him and teach her all the things that were playing in his mind right now, he wasn't going to. They had to live in each other's pockets for twelve months. He was her guardian, he reminded himself rather desperately. He respected her too much to cheapen their relationship with casual sex. He was almost thirty years old and he'd learned by now that sex without commitment wasn't all it was cracked up to be. He didn't love Faith that way and though he wanted her badly, he didn't want to mislead her. She was so innocent she'd probably confuse sex with love. Which wasn't what was between them. Not at all.

Love wasn't an emotion with which he was familiar. In fact, he was pretty sure it didn't exist, except in poets' imaginations. It was just a pretty word to dress up desire. Physical attraction. He'd never seen two people in love yet who weren't physically attracted to each other, proving his point. And when that attraction wore off, there often wasn't enough basic compatibility to keep them together. His parents were a prime example of that.

Things were strained between them during the rest of the evening, though he doubted anyone else would notice. Faith dutifully smiled and made small talk as he took her around the room to introduce her to a few more people who would be offended if he didn't. But she didn't meet his eyes. He kept a hand at the small of her back or lightly around her waist most of the time, just for show.

She was still silent on the drive home.

He said good-night to her at the foot of the stairs, then left her to rustle up the stairs in her pretty gown alone while he moved into his study on the pretext of checking his e-mail. In truth, he didn't really want to be in his room, imagining her disrobing just on the other side of an unlocked door. He trusted his willpower but there was no sense in being stupid.

She was young and beautiful, slim and warm, and his body knew she was available.

Just say no, he reminded himself. He'd seen Nancy Reagan's famous slogan, intended to help kids resist drugs, plastered on billboards. Somehow, it seemed appropriate under the circumstances.

Two weeks passed. Forty-nine more weeks with Stone after this one, she thought to herself one Wednesday morning. Although that time would do her little good, she thought morosely, when the man barely set foot in the same room with her. He left for work at dawn and often worked well past the dinner hour. She'd eaten dinner with her mother and Clarice almost every night and kept a plate warm in the oven for him. Her days were incredibly long and, well, boring.

The one bright spot in the tedium of her current situation was the time she got to spend with her mother. Yesterday, they'd gone across Central Park to the West Side and toured part of the Natural History Museum. Naomi's face had been one big smile the whole time, although Faith worried a little bit that the trip was too tiring for her.

"Tiring?" her mother had said. "How can it be tiring? All I'm doing is driving this scooter."

But privately, Faith could see that her mother had lost a lot of ground in the past year. She was unable to get from bed or chair to her scooter without Faith's or Clarice's assistance. Eating was becoming more difficult due to the tremors that often shook her hands and arms. And on Monday, they'd taken her to the ophthalmologist because Naomi had thought she needed stronger glasses. The ophthalmologist did give her a new prescription, but while she was picking out new frames with Clarice, he'd taken Faith aside and told her that her mother was developing double vision, a common problem with MS. She should see her primary care physician, he'd emphasized, since there were advances in medicine all the time and he didn't know that much about multiple sclerosis.

The worries about her mother's health made every moment they spent together even more special. She thought of Stone, and the way he'd reacted to his mother, and she remembered what he'd said: *Would it have killed her to let a little kid think he meant something special to her?* His resentment was deep-seated and not without cause. But she'd also seen the pain in Eliza's eyes on more than one occasion when Stone had brushed her off. Whatever she'd been or done in the past, she cared about him. And Faith couldn't imagine that a woman who cared about her child would absent herself from his life for extended periods without good reason.

Acting on impulse, she went to the kitchen and found the telephone book, then placed a call. A few moments and two receptionists later, she was speaking with her mother-in-law.

"Faith! What a pleasant surprise!" The CEO of Smythe Corp. sounded delighted to hear from her. "How are you adjusting to marriage?"

"Quite well, thank you." Dangerous subject. She'd better move to the reason for her call. "I was hoping you could join us for lunch one day soon if you're not too busy."

There was a momentary silence on the other end.

"I would love to," Eliza said, and Faith could tell she meant it. "When and what time?"

On Saturday night, Faith and Stone attended the opening of a new Broadway show in the Marriott Marquis. It was a stirring musical based on the life of Abraham Lincoln. It ended with shocking effect with the shot that took Lincoln's life and the audience held their applause for a hushed moment of silence before breaking into wild clapping.

Faith wore another of the dresses Stone had purchased for her and the sapphires again. Might as well let him get his money's worth. She felt constrained in his presence tonight, all too aware of the distance he insisted on imposing. He'd been that way in the weeks since the WARR ball, staying so busy she barely saw him, spending what time he was at home in his office working. Some days she hadn't seen him at all. Others, he'd made charming small talk with her mother and Clarice over dinner, including Faith just enough to make a good showing for the older women. She resented it, but she knew she had no real reason to complain. This was the bargain they'd made. He was living up to his end and expected her to do the same.

"Well," Stone said as they moved toward the room where a private reception to celebrate the opening night was being held, "I predict a long and healthy run." He didn't meet her eyes, though, as he spoke, and she was all too aware this was a public performance.

"I agree." She pointed as they entered the ballroom. "Oh, look at the ice sculpture." There were several stations scattered around the room for hors d'oeuvres and at each one was a towering ice sculpture. The one nearest them was a stunningly faithful representation of Lincoln in profile.

They got plates of pretty sandwiches and other bite-size morsels and Stone brought her a glass of club soda as she'd requested. But he didn't sit down when he returned with her drink. "I see some people I need to speak to," he told her. "I'll be back in a few minutes."

"Oh, I'll go with you." She started to rise, but he put a hand on her shoulder.

"No, it's business. Go ahead and eat. We'll dance when I get back."

She watched him walk away through the crowd. *It's business.* He was determined to keep that part of his life separate from her, it seemed. And to keep himself away as much as possible, too. She ate, and waited. And waited some more. She was getting quite tired of waiting when she saw a small knot of people off to her left. As she scrutinized the group, she realized that they were clustered around a youngish looking dark-haired man. And a moment later, she recognized him as one of the actors from the play.

Well. If Stone wasn't going to entertain her, she'd find someone to talk to on her own. She might never have had the nerve to approach the actor if there hadn't been a ring of fans already around him, but she'd been quite impressed with his performance and wanted to tell him so. Rising, she walked toward the crowd and waited patiently as person after person shook the actor's hand and effused about the show. The man glanced up, and his gaze sharpened as he caught her eye. She smiled and extended her hand.

"I wanted to tell you what a fine performance you gave tonight. I suspect this will keep you employed for quite some time."

The actor laughed, displaying dimples and perfect white teeth. "That would be nice!" He didn't let go of her hand, but turned, tucking it through his arm. "I'm starving. Will you accompany me to the buffet?"

She allowed him to turn her in the right direction.

"What's your name? I'm at a disadvantage—you know mine." His blue eyes twinkled as he looked down at her.

And indeed she did. "I'm Faith," she said. "Faith—Lachlan."

"It's nice to meet you, Faith. Please tell me you aren't here with anyone."

Vaguely alarmed, she released his arm. "Sorry," she said. "My husband is here with me."

"He doesn't seem to be taking very good care of you."

"He is now."

Faith jumped and half turned. Stone had approached behind her. His voice was distinctly chilly. She felt his left hand settle at her waist; the right he extended to the other man. "Stone Lachlan. I take it you've met my wife."

"Sorry," said the actor, backing away, a wry grin on his face. "She was alone. I assumed she was single because no man in his right mind would leave a woman like her alone…" and he turned and headed in the other direction.

Stone's hand slid from her waist and he braceleted her wrist with hard fingers. "Dance with me."

"All right." But he was practically dragging her toward the dance floor.

"Did you tell him," he said through gritted teeth as he swung her into dance position, "that in eleven more months you'll be free to flirt with anyone you want?"

What? She was so shocked by the unexpected attack that she was speechless as he took her in his arms and began to move across the dance floor. "I wasn't—"

"Save it for later, when we don't have an audience," he said curtly.

"I will not!" Finding her voice as outrage rose, she stopped dancing, forcing him to halt as well.

"Faith, you're making a scene." His voice was tight.

"Maybe you should have thought of that before you started slinging around unfair accusations." She tugged at his arm around her waist but it was like pulling on a steel bar. He didn't give an inch. "Let me go," she said. "I want to go home."

"Fine. We'll go home."

"I said I, not we." To her utter mortification, tears rose in her eyes. "I did nothing to deserve to be treated like that. Let me go!"

"Faith—" He hesitated and there was an odd note in his voice. "Don't cry."

"I'm not crying. I'm *furious!*" But that wasn't strictly true. She was devastated that he would accuse her of such a low action. "I wasn't flirting. And if you didn't want me talking to other people, you shouldn't have left me sitting alone for an hour."

She tried to wrench herself away from him but instead of releasing her, Stone merely wrapped his

arms around her and lifted her off her feet, moving
from the dance floor to a partially private spot beside
a large pillar. "Baby," he said roughly, "I'm
sorry—"

"Not as sorry as I am," she said. She deliberately
made her voice and her face expressionless, retreat-
ing in the only way she knew how, forcing herself
to ignore his big, hard body so intimately pressed to
her own.

"Look," he said desperately, "I was wrong. I was
jealous and I didn't handle it very well. Please don't
cry." And before she could evade him, he bent his
head and covered her lips with his.

She'd longed for his kisses, dreamed of them constantly. As his warm mouth moved persuasively on
hers, she tried to hold onto her anger but it was
quickly overridden by her body's clamoring response
to the man she loved. With a small whimper, she put
her arms around his neck and tried to drag him
closer, and between that heartbeat and the next, the
kiss changed. Stone growled deep in his throat and
his arms tightened. He slid one hand down her back
to press her up against him and she gasped as his
tongue slipped along the line of her lips.

Oh, she wanted him! Her pulse beat wildly at the
realization that he wanted her, too. *I was jealous...*
The husky words echoed in her head, melting her
anger and softening her heart as wonder stole in.
He'd been jealous. She could hardly credit that in
light of the way he'd been carefully avoiding any
contact with her, but...he was *kissing* her now, his
mouth moving possessively, his big hands splayed
over her body, holding her tightly against him.

But in a moment, he began to lessen his grip and

his kisses became shallower and more conventional. "My wife," he murmured against her lips as he finally set her free. "You're *my* wife."

His wife…was that all she was to him? Her rising hopes crashed into a flaming abyss once again. Had he only kissed her to establish a claim? To show the world that she was his?

She couldn't quite let herself believe that, not after that kiss. She looked up at him, but he already was leading her out of the ballroom, claiming their coats, hailing a taxi and bundling her in. As he tipped the parking attendant who'd gotten the cab and slid in beside her, she cleared her throat. "Stone?"

"Hmm?"

"Where do we go from here?"

He looked at her questioningly. "Home."

"No." She waited until he braked at a red light and she caught his eye again. "I mean, you and I. Our relationship."

"Faith." His gaze slid back to the street and his voice was firm and resolute. "We've had this discussion before."

"Yes, but—"

"The answer is no. It doesn't matter what you want, or what I want. It would be a huge mistake for us to get involved in a physical relationship."

"Are you trying to convince me or yourself?" she challenged, frustrated beyond belief by his hard-headed refusal to see what they could have together.

"Both, probably," he said grimly.

Six

"Hello, Faith. Thank you for inviting me." Eliza Smythe entered the foyer two weeks later and handed Faith her coat and handbag. "I've been hoping we could get to know each other better."

"So have I," Faith responded, leading her mother-in-law into the dining room, where she had set two places at a small round table near the fireplace. "Please, sit down." She waited until the older woman was seated before she took her own place. "I'm so sorry Stone couldn't be here. He had some pressing things to take care of at his office."

"Pressing things?" Eliza laughed cynically. "I bet they became a whole lot more pressing when he found out I was coming for lunch."

Faith felt herself flushing. She was unable to deny it.

Eliza leaned forward, her face growing serious. "I

hope your invitation didn't cause trouble between
you and Stone.''

"It didn't." That was perfectly truthful. For there
to be trouble between them, they first would have to
talk. Stone's only reaction, when she'd told him his
mother would be coming to lunch was a curt, "I have
meetings all day, so count me out." Gee, what a
shock.

"Good." Faith's mother-in-law smiled warmly at
her. "So tell me how you like married life. Has the
press been too intrusive?"

"Not as bad as I feared, actually," Faith confessed. "But Stone has taught me to keep a low profile in public. That's helped."

"He'll be less interesting now that he's married,"
predicted Eliza. "Unless," she added, smiling wick-
edly, "you keep giving them moments like those
photos from the Lincoln reception. That was hardly
what I'd call low-profile."

Faith felt the heat rise in her face. The week after
the disastrous evening, there had been a series of
three photos of them in the Star Tracks section of
People magazine. In the first frame, Faith was with
the actor she'd met, with her arm tucked warmly
through his. The man's head was tilted down so that
he could hear something she was saying. It was a
decidedly intimate-looking pose.

The second photo showed Stone, scowling, pulling
her toward the dance floor and the other man could
clearly be seen walking away in the background. But
the third shot was the one that had made her cringe.
It had been taken during their heated kiss behind the
pillar. Stone had her locked against him, nearly bent
backward beneath the force of his kiss. She clung to

him on tiptoe, one hand in his hair. The sly, amusing captions had mentioned his jealous reaction—and she doubted the author would ever know how true it had been. Unfortunately, she thought, Stone hadn't been reacting out of any personal feeling. He just didn't want anyone coming on to his wife. She was pretty sure he viewed her as an extension of property.

She ducked her head. "Stone wasn't very happy with that," she admitted. "We'll have to be more careful in the future." Her mother-in-law was still smiling, though, and she decided that the revealing photos probably had helped Stone's cause in his quest to convince his mother of the authenticity of his marriage.

Faith picked up a spoon then and started on the soup she'd set out for the first course. Her mother-in-law followed suit and they talked of other things during the meal. Eliza asked after Faith's mother, and Faith found herself sharing some of her concerns about the future. To her pleasure, Eliza spoke freely about her business. If only Stone would do the same! She longed to share his life, but it seemed he was never going to give her the chance.

"So," the older woman said as they relaxed with coffee an hour later, "we got sidetracked after I asked you how you liked married life. Has it been a big adjustment?"

"In some ways." Faith hesitated, then decided it wouldn't be inappropriate to share her feelings with her mother-in-law. "The boredom is driving me crazy," she confessed, "if you want the truth. I can only spend so much time with Mama—she needs a lot of rest and quiet."

"I thought you were a student. Don't you have classes?"

"I took this semester off." Faith doubted Eliza even knew about Stone taking on financial responsibility for two additional people. In any case, she couldn't explain the details of her "semester off" without the risk of giving away the true reasons for her marriage. "My classes don't start again until June."

"That's not so far away," Eliza pointed out.

Faith raised her eyebrows. "You wouldn't say that if you were the one sitting here twiddling your thumbs. I've asked Stone if I could help at the office but—" she rolled her eyes and tried to sound mildly aggravated as an indulgent wife might "—he told me to redecorate the den." Her opinion of *that* was evident in her voice.

"Well, it is a project," his mother said, playing devil's advocate.

"One I accomplished in a few days," Faith said. "The painters are here right now. The wallpaper, carpet and new furniture have been ordered."

Eliza chuckled. "And you're twiddling your thumbs again." As Faith nodded, the older woman cleared her throat. "I might have a project for you, if you're interested."

A project? Faith was cautious. "Such as?"

"I have a significant amount of data from one of my plants that recently was restructured. The last man was an incompetent idiot and he left a huge mess with a number of damaged files that need to be recovered. It needs to be straightened out. It would be a short-term job, of course, but it might be perfect for your situation."

Faith's spirits soared immediately. She nearly clapped her hands. Then something occurred to her. "Wait a minute. How do you know I'm capable of doing this job?"

Eliza's slim shoulders rose and fell in a wry gesture. "I confess I did look into your background a little bit. You have quite a gift with computers, it seems."

She didn't know whether to be flattered or annoyed. "I'm beginning to see where Stone gets his autocratic nature."

Her mother-in-law winced. "I'm sorry if I've made you angry."

"It's all right." She wasn't really angry. "The job sounds like a challenge. I like challenges. But I'll need to talk to Stone about it."

"All right." Eliza rose. "Thank you for lunch. Whether or not you take the job, I hope we can continue to get together from time to time."

"That would be nice." And it would be. "Perhaps Stone will be able to join us next time."

Eliza made a distinctly unladylike sound. "Not if he finds out I'm going to be there."

The words were filled with pain, as were her eyes. Faith hesitated. She knew Stone wouldn't thank her for getting in the middle of his relationship with his mother...still, she couldn't simply ignore this. "I'm sorry," she said. "Maybe, in time, he'll soften." But she doubted it.

Eliza sighed. "You don't believe that and neither do I. Stone thinks I abandoned him. And he's right. I did." Her face looked as rigid as marble. The only sign of life was the leaping, snapping flames in her eyes. "When my father died, I was a young wife with a small child. And suddenly, I was the heir to this company—which was struggling to keep its head above water, something my father had never told me. I was determined to keep Smythe for my son. Maybe I should have hired someone else to lead it, but at the time I felt like…oh, I don't know, like it was my destiny or something." She tried to smile. "Or maybe it just makes me feel better to tell myself I had no other choice but to take over and lead the company myself."

"It must have been a good decision," Faith said, realizing what a difficult choice Eliza had been forced to make. "Look at what you've accomplished."

The Smythe Corp. CEO shrugged. "But look at what I sacrificed. My marriage fell apart when my husband realized I had no intention of walking away from Smythe Corp. I should have refused to cooperate when he told me to leave. I should have taken Stone with me. But he was so close to his father…I didn't think it would be fair." She shook her head. "Of course, I never thought my husband would try to keep me from seeing my son, either. And once I'd moved out, the courts *did* view me as a poor parent." Her shoulders slumped. "I guess we all have things we wish we had done differently."

Faith was stunned. Stone thought his mother hadn't wanted him! All these years he'd thought she didn't care…he couldn't have been more wrong.

"You, ah, wanted to see him more often?"

His mother looked beaten. "Yes, but when his father got full custody he was able to severely limit the time I spent with Stone. After a while, Stone seemed to view my visits as a chore and it was easier not to go as often." She shook her head regretfully. "I'm very sorry now that I didn't continue to be a presence in Stone's life no matter what."

Then she glanced at her watch, and Faith could see her shaking off the moment of painful truth. "I have enjoyed this tremendously, Faith. Thank you again for inviting me. It's time for me to get back to the office."

"Thank you for joining me." Faith rose and laid her napkin aside, then led the way to the front door.

Eliza put on her coat, then turned once more. "Let me know if you're interested in that job. It wouldn't just be something I've made up to keep you busy. I really do need to get someone on that project soon."

"I'll let you know by the end of the week," Faith promised. "I appreciate the offer more than you know."

She was just coming down the stairs to breakfast two days later when she heard Stone calling her name. His voice sounded alarmed, unusual for him, and immediately she doubled her speed.

He was in the breakfast room. So was her mother. But Naomi was lying on the floor near the table with him crouched at her side.

"Mama!" Faith rushed forward, taking in the scene. Her mother was conscious, though she lay awkwardly on her side. "What happened?"

"She says she was transferring from her scooter to the table. She had a muscle spasm and she slipped," Stone said. As Faith dropped to her knees, Stone rose and left the room, returning a moment later with the telephone as well as a blanket, which he draped over her mother. "It's a good thing it's

Saturday," he said, "or I might not still have been home. She could have lain here for a while except that I was in the kitchen and I heard her."

"Where's Clarice? And why were you trying to do this alone?" Faith knew her voice was too shrill but she was frightened. Naomi shouldn't have been trying to move without supervision.

Clarice had agreeably offered to work six days a week. Sunday was the only day she took off and even then, she often was gone only a few hours. She had no children and, Faith assumed, no other family.

"I sent her to the deli," said Naomi. "They have wonderful fresh bagels. I thought I could...I thought..." Her voice trailed off and she started to cry.

"It's okay, Mama." Faith stroked her hair. "It's okay. How do you feel? Do you think anything is broken?"

"Don't try to move." Stone's voice brooked no opposition. "Let me call an ambulance and we'll go to the hospital so you can be checked."

"No emergency service," Naomi begged.

Stone shook his head as he punched a speed dial button. "I won't call 9-1-1. I'm calling your doctor first."

Clarice returned just as Stone hung up from explaining the situation to Naomi's doctor. The caregiver was as upset as Faith had ever seen her, and it was as much work to calm Clarice as it was to comfort her mother. Things moved rapidly after that. Naomi's doctor sent a private ambulance and she was transported to the hospital where she was met by her doctor. Faith, Stone and Clarice waited impatiently until a nurse appeared to take them to the room in which they'd settled Naomi.

The doctor who oversaw her care met them in the hallway and took all three of them into a small visitors' lounge before they saw Faith's mother.

"Your mother is experiencing an increase in spasticity that worries me. It's important that we begin a physical therapy program in order to keep it from worsening. Passive stretching, maybe some swimming, that kind of thing. Also, she absolutely should not attempt transfers from one place to another without physical assistance. Sometimes the spasms can be severe enough to knock a patient right out of their wheelchair."

"Is she going to have to start using a wheelchair now?" Faith asked apprehensively.

"I'm not ready to take that step yet," the doctor replied. "Let's see if we can't control the spasticity first."

"Exactly what do you want us to do?" Stone's voice was authoritative and Faith was happy to let him direct the conversation.

"I would recommend one of two things: either hire trained therapists who can work with Mrs. Harrell, or consider placing her in a facility where she can be cared for."

"You mean a nursing home," Faith said dully. She'd worried about this edict for years. Now, suddenly, here it was. And she was no closer to accepting it than she had been before.

"She won't need a nursing home." Stone put his arm comfortingly around her shoulder as he addressed the doctor. "But if you could give us the names of some reliable sources of personnel, we'll get more help at home."

Stunned, Faith stared at him and he glanced down at her and smiled.

A moment later, the doctor left.

Clarice rose. "I guess you won't need me now," she said in a small voice. "I don't know how to help her exercise."

"Oh, you're not getting away from us," Stone told her in a firm voice, removing his arm from around Faith and standing. He took Clarice's hands in his. "Unless you want to, that is. Naomi depends on you, and so do Faith and I. If you agree to stay, you'll be in charge of any personnel who come in to help. It'll be your job to make sure they're doing theirs, and that everything is going smoothly."

Clarice stared at Stone for a long moment. She opened her mouth, but no sound came out. Faith realized the older woman was on the verge of tears. Finally she said, "Thank you. Thank you so much. I don't have any family and I've gotten really fond of Naomi. I would have hated leaving all of you."

"And we would hate to lose you," Faith said, rising and hugging the older lady. "We're your family now."

Clarice went ahead of them to see Naomi as Faith turned to Stone. She swallowed with difficulty and took a deep breath. "I appreciate your support but I know you hadn't counted on this when we made our agreement. I won't hold you to anything you said to that doctor."

"I know you won't. But I still intend to hire additional help and keep your mother in our home."

"You've done enough for us already," she told

him unsteadily. "I don't think your father meant for you to support us for the rest of our natural lives." She tried to smile at the weak joke.

Stone put his arms around her and pulled her head to his shoulder, just holding her for a long, sweet moment. "Your mother means a lot to me, too," he told her. "She and Clarice have made the house a warmer, livelier place."

She pulled back and searched his gaze for a long moment. He appeared to be completely serious. "Thank you." She didn't know how she ever would repay him, but she would swallow her pride to make sure her mother was happy and well-cared-for. Putting Naomi in a nursing home would have been devastating for her as well as for Faith.

"Don't thank me," he said, still holding her loosely in his arms. "I mean it. Keeping her at home is really an act of selfishness on my part."

"Right." Although she could have stayed in the comforting embrace forever, she forced herself to move away from him. "You're a good man," she said quietly, touching his cheek with a gentle hand before turning to leave the room.

They visited briefly with her mother. She hadn't been badly hurt, just severely bruised and she'd broken a bone in her wrist. She would be staying overnight at the hospital for some additional tests and would be released tomorrow. Faith was relieved the fall hadn't been worse.

Clarice decided to stay at the hospital for a few hours and told them she would take a cab home later. On the ride home, Stone said, "I haven't told you how good the den looks. I really like my new chair." He flexed his fingers on the wheel. "I believe my mother must have chosen the old furnishings. I don't ever remember it looking any different.''

"Your mother did a lovely job," she told him. "The things she chose lasted a long time."

"Longer than she did."

"I'm not sure that was her choice, entirely." It was a risk, talking about his mother, but she felt she had to try to share with him his mother's version of the past.

The car was uncomfortably quiet for a moment. Then he said, "It's old news." He shrugged, frowning as he drove. "Who cares anymore?"

You do. "She does," Faith said. "She didn't want to leave you behind but your father fought her for custody. And limited her visits. She's always wanted to be a bigger part of your life than she was permitted to be."

"And I suppose she told you this during your cozy little luncheon." His voice was expressionless.

"Yes." There was another awkward silence. She waited for him to ask her what she meant, what his mother had said. But he never did.

Instead he finally said, "We got off the track, I believe. We were talking about the changes in the den."

"I'm glad you like the new look and the new furniture." She was disappointed that he hadn't listened to more of his mother's story, but at least he hadn't bitten her head off. "I really wasn't sure about it, but since you told me to go ahead..." Then she followed up on the opening he'd given her. She'd been trying to figure out a way to approach him again for several days. "Now that the job is finished, I'm finding myself with a lot of free time. You know, I'm not sure you appreciate the extent of my computer skills. Surely there's something at your company that I could—"

"There really isn't," he interrupted her. "But I did want to ask you to do something else." Without giving her a chance to respond, he said, "I've received several wedding gifts at the office and I know we've begun to get quite a few more at the house. Would you please write thank-you notes to everyone? I'll supply you with the addresses you need."

"I've kept a list of everything. The files are on the computer in your home office," she told him, disappointment shading her tone. "I'd thought perhaps it was something we could do together."

But he shook his head. "I really don't have the time. I'm sorry. At the end of the week I'll be leaving for China for a nine-day trip."

"China!" She couldn't believe he hadn't mentioned this before. How long had he intended to wait before telling her?

"Yes. We have an incredible opportunity to get our foot in the door with some steel exports." Unaware of her thoughts, he sounded as excited as she had ever heard him. "And I want to investigate the possibilities of setting up an American division of Lachlan Industries in Beijing."

It had been a strange conversation. He'd taken her to the heights of exasperation but now he was sharing his business plans with her...something she'd wanted for so long. Cautiously, afraid he would clam up again, she said. "Lachlan Industries in Beijing?"

"Uh-huh. The world really has become a global marketplace. If I want Lachlan to be a player on more than a national level, I have to establish a pres-

ence around the world. Our plants in Germany pro-
duce a number of products for the European market.
One in Beijing could serve a sizable portion of the
Far East, including Taiwan and Japan.'' He was
warming to his theme and his tone was enthusiastic.

"Now I understand why people say you have the
Midas touch,'' she said. "You never stop thinking
of ways to improve.''

"I can't,'' he said simply, "if I want to stay on
top. I'm always looking for the next opportunity. It's
a full-time effort.''

"When you take over your mother's corporation,
how will you manage both companies?''

Instantly the light in his eyes flattened and cooled.
She saw immediately that she'd said the wrong thing.
He shrugged, elaborately casual. "I'll probably work
out some kind of merger. Get everything under one
umbrella so I don't have so many balls to juggle.''

His too-casual tone, coupled with an explanation
that sounded wooden and rehearsed, alerted her to
the realization that this wasn't just business for
Stone. Merge the two companies?

Some of the pieces of the puzzle that was her husband clicked into place as she recalled the odd note
of near-desperation in his tone on the night he'd laid
out his proposal. Her heart ached for him as a flash
of insight showed her the truth. He didn't want
Smythe Corp. because it was a good deal, or even
because it was a family tradition. A merger was
something he could control as he hadn't been able to
control the disintegration of his family when he'd
been a child—and in a very tangible if symbolic
sense, he would be putting his family back together
again.

She wondered if he understood that some things could never be fixed. Quietly she said, "You know, merging these companies is nice, but it isn't going to help you resolve your differences with your mother. You really ought to sit down and talk with her."

But she could tell her impassioned words had fallen on deaf ears. His face drained of expression and when he looked at her, his eyes were as cool as the blustery spring weather outside. "Funny, but I don't remember asking you for your opinion on what I ought to do with my mother. All I require of you is that you play a part for ten more months."

She felt as though he'd slapped her. As a reminder of the time limit she had, it was fairly brutal. She didn't speak again, and when they arrived home, she got out of the car before he could open her door and hurried inside, heading for her room. *Fine,* she thought angrily. *Let him go to China. Let him count down the days until he rids himself of me. Let him refuse to give me anything meaningful to do.*

With that thought, she remembered Eliza's offer. And she reached for the phone.

"This place is awesome!" Faith's former roommate Gretchen bounced into the kitchen of the town house as they completed a short tour of the house several days later. She turned to face Faith, her expressive pixie face alight. "I still can't believe you're married to him."

"I can't believe it, either," Faith said wryly. "It's a little overwhelming sometimes."

"He's really been great about your mom living here." Gretchen flung herself onto one of the bar stools. "Tim would wig out if I asked him to let my mother live with us."

"It's a slightly different situation." Faith felt compelled to defend Gretchen's steady beau, one of the nicest guys she'd ever met. "I mean, it's not as though we're tripping over each other like we would in a small place."

"Yeah, I guess the money makes a difference." The redhead made a little moue of frustration. "Money. I wish it didn't exist."

"Amen." Gretchen couldn't know how much Faith meant that. Then her friend's woebegone expression registered, and she focused on Gretchen. "What's wrong?"

Gretchen shrugged. "Nothing, really. Tim asked me to marry him—"

"When? Why didn't you tell me?" Faith leaped from her own seat and embraced her friend. "Congratulations!"

But Gretchen raised a hand and indicated that she should calm down. "Well, frankly, it isn't that big a deal yet. Tim says he wants to marry me, but he wants us to save some money first. He's thinking we should buy a house in New Jersey."

"And you don't want to do that?"

"Are you kidding? I'd love it!" Gretchen waved her hands about. "Big old trees, a little white picket fence and a house with shutters. We could get a dog…we've even talked about children." Her big eyes sparkled with tears. "But he wants to wait until we can make a down payment on a home to get married. I love the stupid man and I want to marry him *now!*"

"Why should you wait?" Faith tried to think

about it from Tim's point of view. And failed. People who loved each other should marry. What did money have to do with love?

"Beats me."

"I don't get it, either." Faith sighed heavily. "I'm sorry. Men are such dolts sometimes."

"You said it, girlfriend." Shedding her sad mood, Gretchen eyed Faith over the rim of her coffee cup. "That sounded like you had one specific man in mind."

Faith smiled slightly. "Without question."

"Problems with the tycoon?"

"A few." If her friend only knew!

"Sex," said Gretchen.

Faith nearly choked on the coffee she'd just swallowed. "What?"

"Men are amazingly easy to manipulate if you start with a little physical T.L.C."

"They are not."

"That's what all the magazines say." And that, as far as Gretchen was concerned, made it fact. "So you just have to dazzle him with incredible, unforgettable sex and then talk about whatever's bothering you. He'll be much more malleable then."

"You are *terrible!*" Faith began to giggle as she saw the glint of humor lurking in her friend's eyes. But her amusement faded away as she thought about her marriage. "Anyway, that's not an option. We don't—" Oh, my God. She stopped, appalled at her runaway tongue.

Gretchen was staring at her as if she'd sprouted a second head. "Tell me you are kidding. You have a platonic relationship with one of the most gorgeous men in North America?"

"Um, yes, that's about right." Faith squirmed beneath the incredulous stare.

"Don't you love him?"

Faith nodded sadly. "I do. I never knew it was possible to care for someone the way I care for him. But that doesn't mean it's mutual."

"Well, if he doesn't love you and you're not having wild, bed-wrecking sex every night, then why the heck did he *marry* you?"

Well, there was no backing out of it now. If there was a more persistent woman than her redheaded friend on the face of the planet, Faith would have to meet her to be convinced. "He married me because he feels responsible for me," she said miserably. To an extent, that was true, and it was the only thing she could say to her friend without breaking Stone's trust. "His father and mine were best friends. When they were killed together, Stone became my guardian."

"Your *guardian?* How Victorian!" Gretchen's eyes were wide. "And because of that he felt compelled to marry you?" Her eyes narrowed and she gave a snort of disbelief. "Uh-uh. I don't buy it."

"It's true," Faith said glumly. "That's why we haven't—we don't—"

"Give me a break." Gretchen hopped off her stool and paced around the kitchen. "Look me in the eye and tell me that if you were as homely as a mud fence he'd have married you." When Faith's brow wrinkled and she hesitated, Gretchen stabbed her index finger at her. "See? I knew it! No man would sacrifice himself like that. He wants you."

"He doesn't." Faith stopped, remembering the

passionate kisses they'd shared, and her expression reflected her lack of conviction.

"Ha! I knew it." Gretchen was grinning at the look on her friend's face. "He *does* want you. He's just trying to be, I don't know, noble or something. I guess he's got some hang-up about that guardian stuff. Still…if he's hot for you, there's hope. You just have to seduce him."

"*Seduce him?* You are insane."

"No, no, I'm serious." And her freckled face did look surprisingly sober. "I might have been kidding before, but I am so totally not joking about this. Faith, you were meant to be with this guy. And he was meant to love you back. He's just too dumb to know it. You're going to have to go after him big time."

"No way." She shook her head, remembering the way he'd rejected her before, and the way he'd reacted two days ago when she'd tried to encourage him to mend his fences with his mother. "He's made it clear what his position is."

"Oh, come on. Aren't you the girl who came to town without a job *or* a place to live, and found both the very first day? If you really want him, he's toast. You just have to go for it."

"This is a ridiculous conversation." Faith rose and began stacking dishes. "Come on, I'll take you in to meet my mother and her companion before you have to get back."

But Gretchen's words lingered in her mind long after her old roommate had left. *If he's hot for you, there's hope.*

Seven

The trip to China lasted three days longer than he'd planned. By the time Stone left LaGuardia behind and slipped his key into the lock of his town house, he was exhausted. The meetings had been long and ultimately fairly successful from a business standpoint. But the strain inherent in communicating his ideas effectively to people of another culture had worn him down. But it wasn't only that. For the first time in his life, he'd been impatient to conclude his business and get home. Not so that he could get back to work, but so he could get *home*.

Impatient. Right. How about so nervous he couldn't even spit? He checked his watch. It was nearly ten in the evening. He'd been away for twelve days and they'd seemed like twelve hundred.

He'd hated traveling. No, he thought, trying to be honest. He'd hated traveling alone. God, he'd never imagined feeling lonely simply because a certain woman wasn't at his side. He'd never expected to be seized with a barely controllable urge to hop a flight and fly home simply because that's where she was. He'd never, *ever* thought about a woman so much that it shattered his concentration and turned his brain to mush in the middle of important meetings.

But thoughts of Faith had done all that to him and more. He'd lain awake aching for her, knowing that even if he were in New York he'd still be aching for her…and wishing he were there, anyway, because then at least he'd be close to her.

He must have been crazy when he'd married her, he decided as he took the stairs two at a time. How could any man be expected to ignore the temptation of her lithe young body day after day after day? It was natural for him to want her, to ache for her. It was just a physical reaction.

He walked through the house, noting the lamp that was always lit now in the hallway that led to the kitchen. Faith had begun leaving it on for Clarice, in case she came to get something from the kitchen at night. He'd gotten used to seeing the small glow.

He walked down the hallway to his bedroom door, noting that Faith's was firmly closed. Would she come to greet him when she heard him moving around? Probably not. He'd have to wait until morning.

Morning. He realized he'd actually missed mornings at home. On the days he hadn't run from the house at dawn, he'd shared breakfast with Faith and sometimes her mother and Clarice. He'd always imagined he'd find having other people around first thing in the morning annoying, but it was surprisingly pleasant.

It might not be so pleasant now, after the way he'd left things with Faith. But even then, knowing that she was likely to be cool and formal with him, something eased in his chest because at long last he was home again, and she was sleeping right in the next room. He hoped he could make things right with her. He missed her smile, and the habit she had of humming beneath her breath as she moved around the house.

She hadn't done much humming the past few days before he'd gone to China. Their parting had been strained, stiff, the way things had been between them since the day of her mother's accident. He should have apologized for the things he'd said to her about her interference with his mother. Faith had a good heart and a wonderful relationship with her own mother; it probably was beyond her capabilities to understand the way he felt.

He stepped into his bedroom and dropped his suitcase inside the door. A startled squeak made him jerk his head around to locate the source—and there she stood.

She must have just finished in the shower because she had a towel wrapped around her torso and her hair was pinned atop her head. He could see droplets of water gleaming on her shoulders.

Immediately he felt a rush of desire begin to radiate through his body, making him take a short, tense breath as every inch of his skin seemed to sizzle with an electric charge. He'd been thinking of her, wanting her for so long that it only took moments to make him worry that she'd notice the burgeoning arousal pushing at the front of his pants.

"Hello," he said, and his voice was husky. "I didn't mean to scare you."

"It's all right." She smiled at him, and the radiance of her expression tightened every muscle in his body. "I'm glad you're home. I missed you."

"I, uh, missed you, too." He couldn't look away from her. She was smiling, her gray eyes shining, so beautiful that he ached with the need to cross to her and crush her to him. She apparently had forgiven him. Or forgotten their argument. Hah. He doubted Faith would forget something like that.

Then she put her hands up to the top of the tucked-in fabric and his whole body tightened. She took a deep breath, uncertainty flashing in her eyes so fast he wasn't sure he'd seen it to begin with. And before he could say a word, she dropped the towel.

As it fell away from her, he made a strangled sound in his throat. She was as beautiful as all his fevered imaginings, long, slim, sleekly muscled. Her breasts were high and round with deep rosy nipples that puckered beneath his gaze. Her bare feet curled into the carpet and he couldn't prevent his gaze from sliding up her long elegant legs, over the splendid curve of her hip. At the junction of her thighs, a thatch of blond curls protected her deepest secrets.

As he devoured her with his gaze, she fought an obvious battle with shyness and modesty. Her hands came halfway up her body in a defensive posture before she deliberately let them relax at her side again. A rosy blush suffused her neck and climbed into her cheeks, but she held out her arms to him, still smiling into his eyes. "Make love to me."

His blood surged heavily, nearly propelling him into her arms. He wanted her, and he hated himself for it. She was too young.

She's not too young. She's legal.

Well, she was too young for him.

Ten years isn't a huge age gap.

"Stone?" She came through the dividing door into his bedroom and began to walk across the room toward him, her eyes flickering with nerves even though her voice was steady and warm. "This is the part where you're supposed to respond."

She obviously hadn't noticed just how *responsive* he was. He felt himself beginning to sweat. "Dammit, Faith, just stay over there." He backed around the other side of the bed, putting some space between them, appalled at the panicked note in his voice. "You don't want this."

"I do." Her voice was as soft as ever but there was a note of determination in it that shook him. "I thought about it the whole time you were gone. I've been thinking about it since the day you asked me to marry you." She took a deep breath and he couldn't prevent his gaze from dropping to her breasts as the firm mounds rose and fell "I want my first…first time to be with someone I trust and care for. I want it to be with *you.*"

"No, you don't." But her words sent unpleasant images bolting into his mind, images of Faith with another man, and he had to bite back the snarl that wanted to escape.

"I do," she said again. She reached up and took the clip from her hair, tossing it onto his dresser as the silky blond tresses fell down her back and framed her body. She came around the end of the bed and walked to him.

He put out a hand like a traffic cop to hold her off but she slipped inside it and pressed herself against him, her hands sliding up to curl around his neck as her lips grazed the sensitive skin where his shirt collar exposed his throat.

He groaned at the feel of her slim young frame pressed against him. She smelled fresh and sweet, and despite his good intentions, his extended hand dropped to her back, sliding slowly up and down her sleek spine, testing the naked, resilient flesh, moving dangerously down to trace the cleft in her buttocks. His hand clenched spasmodically on her soft flesh, pressing her hips hard against his aching arousal. "We won't be able to get an annulment." His voice sounded hoarse and unfamiliar to his ears.

"I don't care." She kissed his throat again. "How can this be so bad when we both want it so much?"

"I haven't changed my mind about this being a mistake." But he had. The words she'd said, that she wanted *him* to be the one, danced through his head. If he refused...he couldn't even complete the thought. Instead he ran his hands over her silky skin everywhere he could reach, savoring the soft, sweet feel of her as common sense warred with pure carnal need. Finally need won. He dropped his head and sought her mouth, wrapping his arms around her. His kisses were hard and wild, his tongue plunging deep. She gasped and he remembered how innocent she was, so he reined himself in with gargantuan effort, gentling his kisses, stroking the inside surfaces of her mouth with his tongue and teasing her until she followed his lead, her tongue hesitantly joining his, exploring his mouth as fully as he explored hers. Finally he tore his lips from hers, breathing heavily. He kissed her cheek, slid his mouth along her jaw and down the side of her neck. She smelled of scented bath soap and the unique flavor of her silken skin.

He raised his head, capturing her gaze, and his face was rigid with the control he was exerting to rein in the need he felt. "No," he gritted. "I can't do this anymore. I can't fight myself and you both. I can't pretend I don't want to make love to you when every hour of every day, I'm thinking about doing *this*." He slid one hand boldly around to cup her breast and his thumb found the tip of her nipple, rubbing gently back and forth. Her eyes closed as he watched her face, and her lips parted as her breath rushed in and out. Then he bent his head and replaced his thumb with his mouth, suckling her strongly, and her eyes flew wide. Wildly she arched against him as she cried out.

"And this," he muttered against her breast, sliding the same hand down over her rib cage and the softness of her belly, stroking gently before plunging firmly down between her legs to her most intimate feminine secrets. She was moist and slick, surprisingly ready for him. He cupped her, sliding his fingers between her legs as he used his thumb on the small bud hidden beneath the sweet curls. Her body arched again at the new sensation and she gasped. Then she set her hands against his shoulders, trying to push him away, instinctively wary and nervous of such implacable male determination.

"Ah, no, baby, don't fight me." He lifted his head and took her lips again, understanding her momentary panic. Despite her brave invitations, she was still an innocent. The act of giving herself to a man made a woman intensely vulnerable. And so he simply let his hand lay against her as he resumed kissing her until she felt secure with him, permitting him access to her mouth without restraint as her legs relaxed. Then slowly he resumed the intimate caresses. He slid one finger inside her, groaning at the tight, wet feel of her clinging flesh and his hips surged forward as he tried to ease the harsh need driving him. "That's it," he growled. "I want to make you feel good. We're going to be so good together."

Withdrawing his hand from its nest, he slid both arms beneath her and lifted her into his arms, moving the short distance to his bed. She put her arms around his neck and lifted her face to his and he sat down on the side of the bed, kissing her and stroking her, torn between the need to bury himself deeply within her and find release, and the desire to explore her hidden treasures for hours. But then she shifted against him, her hip pressing hard against his full flesh, and he knew he wasn't going to be able to wait hours.

She lifted her hands and inexpertly began to unbutton his shirt. He rose, laying her on the bed, then quickly shed his shirt and jacket in one movement, removing his shoes and socks, taking off his belt, all without taking his eyes from the bounty of her bared body.

She was watching him, too, and he saw her pupils contract as he tore off his shirt. She lifted one hand from the bed and laid it over the rigid, throbbing flesh that distended his pants and he nearly jumped out of his skin. He tore at the fastenings, pushing his trousers down and off along with his briefs. Her eyes widened again as his need for her came fully free, and her gaze flashed to his. "Can I...touch you?" she whispered.

He gritted his teeth at the unconscious sensuality of her request as her body turned toward him. "Sorry, baby." He caught her wrist and linked his fingers with hers. "That would be a really bad idea right now. This would be over before it ever really got started."

She smiled and her voice was nearly a purr when she said, "Then I'll wait."

He came down on the bed beside her, sighing as his naked flesh met hers for the first time. His erection pressed against her hip and he could feel the moisture he couldn't hold back dampening her flesh. He shuddered, hoping he could wait long enough to make it good for her.

Quickly he smoothed his hand down over her downy belly and feathered his fingers over the sweet folds between her legs again. Her gaze was fastened on his and he caught a hint of apprehension in her beautiful eyes. Leaning forward, he kissed each of her eyelids as they fluttered shut. "Relax," he whispered. "I'll take care of you." He leaned over her and took her breast, suckling firmly until she moaned and tried to arch toward him. His fingers grew bolder, parting her and opening her for him, and he shifted his weight onto her, his arms shaking with the effort it took not to simply shove himself into her and ride her until he exploded. But Faith was a virgin. And she was...special. He wanted it to be as good for her as it was going to be for him. He pulled his hips back and let his shaft rub her, then reached down and opened her further until the slightest surge forward caught the head of his aroused flesh within her.

She gasped.

He groaned.

She raised a hand, and wiped away a drop of sweat that trickled down his temple. "Is this hard for you?" she whispered.

He chuckled deep in his throat. "No, it's hard for *you*." Her eyes widened as he probed her, alert to the barrier that signaled her virginity. Just within her, he met resistance. "I'm going to try not to hurt you," he warned her, "but the first time might not be much fun." She watched him wide-eyed as he moved his hand between them and found again the pouting bud he'd exposed. As he began to lightly press and circle, her eyes closed and her back arched, pushing him a little deeper.

"That's—too much," she panted. "I can't…I can't…"

"You can," he breathed. "Let it build, baby." He kept his tone soft, his voice low, watching the flush that spread over her fair skin as she gave herself to her passion, to him. In a moment, her hips began to respond to his encouraging touch, rising and falling, and he had to steel himself to withstand the seductive lure of her body caressing the tip of him.

"Stone," she cried, "hold me!"

"I've got you, baby," he crooned. "Let go, let go, let go…"

And she did. He saw the shock in her eyes as her body convulsed, shuddering beneath him, and as she arched wildly up to meet him, he plunged forward, burying himself deep within her responsive body.

"Oh!" Her legs came up to wrap around his hips,

possibly the most erotic feeling he'd ever known, and as her sweet channel continued to rhythmically caress him, he began to move, stroking heavily in and out, teeth clenched, body shaking. He was so ready that it took only moments until he erupted, falling over the edge into her soft arms as he emptied himself deep, deep within her. Pleasure shattered his senses as it spread throughout every cell in his body, rendering him momentarily deaf and blind.

As he began to regain his senses, he looked down at her. "Are you all right?"

"I'm fine."

"I didn't hurt you?"

"Only a tiny bit." She smiled at him, her fingers rubbing the back of his neck. "You were wrong. The first time *was* fun."

He chuckled as he slowly lowered his weight onto her, conscious of her slight frame. But she kept her legs and arms around him when he would have shifted himself to one side, holding him close until he let himself go boneless in her embrace. He rested his forehead on the pillow next to her and moaned as her fingers lightly kneaded up and down his back.

"Stone?"

"Hmm?" He was so relaxed it was an effort to move enough to reply.

"How long before we can do it again?"

His eyes flew open. He started to laugh, lifting himself on his elbows to inspect her face, then dropping his head to kiss her. "A little while, at least," he told her. "I'm pretty tired. But on second thought—" he moved his hips experimentally "—I'm feeling much more rested already."

She smiled, her gaze warm and contented and he

kissed her again, lingering for a moment before he
levered himself up and began to withdraw—

And froze. He swore vividly, and Faith's eyes widened in shock.

"What?" she demanded.

He pulled himself back to his knees, then stood
and cursed again, his hands on his hips, his still-erect
flesh cooling unpleasantly. "No protection," he said
grimly. "How the hell could I have been that stupid?" he asked the ceiling. But he knew exactly how
stupid he'd been. He'd been so focused on completing the act of making her young, virgin body his that
protection had been the last thing on his mind.

Faith went very still, probably as horrified as he
was. After a moment, she sat up and eased herself to
the side of the bed. Her brow wrinkled momentarily
and she winced; he realized she was feeling some
discomfort. But she stood, and stepped forward to
slide her arms around his waist and press herself
against him.

"It's all right," she said. She kissed his collarbone
and then looked up at him. "I love you. I wouldn't
mind if I got pregnant."

His body had reacted automatically to the soft feel
of her curves but her words were a shock of ice water
on his rising passion. "Faith," he said grimly, taking
her by the shoulders and holding her gently but
firmly away from him, focusing on the only part of
her statement he could allow himself to believe. "*I'd*
mind. This marriage is only going to last a year, remember?"

She simply gazed at him. And he was the first to
look away.

"I know you think you love me," he said, desperate to convince her. "It's natural when two people make love for feelings to get mixed up with basic human needs. But trust me, you won't love me in a year."

Still, she regarded him silently. Finally she opened her mouth. "You're wrong. I'll still love you in a year. I'll still love you in ten years, and in twenty."

"Look," he said, frantic to erase the echo of those seductive words, "let's not get into a fight about this."

She smiled at that, and he stared at her, mystified. What the hell was so funny? "I wasn't planning to fight with you," she said. "I want to make love again." She stepped forward, pressing herself against him, burying her face in his neck. Her warm breath stirred the curls on his chest and he shuddered, knowing that she surely could feel the arousal he couldn't prevent.

"This isn't lovemaking," he said above her head. "This is sex."

"Okay." She nuzzled his chest and he leaped a foot in the air when her lips grazed his nipple. "You call it what you want and I'll call it what I want."

If he was smart, he'd walk away from this right now, and not compound one error by making another. But his arms came around her without his permission, and his head lowered and sought her lips all on its own. His body knew what it wanted even though his mind knew better. "And we use protection," he decreed, trying to retain some control of the situation. She was a twenty-year-old recently deflowered virgin. How could she be so unshakably certain of herself?

"If that's what you want," she said agreeably. Her

small hand slipped slowly down his body and his
stomach muscles contracted sharply. "Is it okay to
touch you now?" she asked.

He closed his eyes and exhaled in surrender.
"Yeah," he said, giving himself to this night and
this moment. He'd worry about tomorrow later. "But
only if I get to touch you, too."

She awoke before dawn, aware of her body in a
way she'd never been before. She lay on her side,
her back cuddled into the living furnace of her husband. Stone's left arm was draped over her hip, the
other was beneath the pillow on which both their
heads lay.

With dreamy satisfaction, she relived the hours
just past. He'd scared her silly when he'd walked into
his bedroom without warning. Even though he'd told
her his flight would be in that night, she hadn't really
expected to see him. He'd warned her that he'd probably get home in the wee hours.

It was probably just as well that he'd surprised her.
If she'd been prepared, she'd never, ever have had
the nerve to approach and seduce him the way she
had! She took a deep breath, remembering the moment of sheer terror she'd felt when she'd decided to
drop her towel and take Gretchen's advice. At first,
she'd thought he really was going to refuse. But then
she'd seen his hands clenched in fists. She'd felt the
barely contained desire he kept on a tight leash and
she'd pushed a little more until the volcano had
erupted and he'd swept over her with the force of a
hot lava flow, incinerating her modesty and her virginity with his sheer delight in her body and his blatant encouragement of her sexuality. She might know

another lover someday, but she knew without question that she'd never meet another man who pleased her like Stone did, who anticipated her every need before she even realized what she wanted.

She loved him so much. He still couldn't let himself see that they were perfect for each other. He'd led her to believe it was because of their age difference but the truth was, Stone was terrified of intimacy. Not physical intimacy, but emotional closeness. She knew he'd had scores of lovers in the past, but she was certain none of them knew him the way she did, knew his secret need for a stable home, the sorrow and resentment that threatened to permanently damage his relationship with his mother, the unacknowledged wish for a family of his own.

A family. A baby. How amazing that she hadn't even been thinking much about that kind of future until he'd introduced the possibility. She'd always thought of herself as a good girl. Going to her marriage bed a virgin was simply a given. But it shook her a little to realize that it wouldn't have mattered if she'd been married to Stone or not. If he'd ever tried to seduce her, he would have had her anytime he'd wanted. And it scared her more than a little that she hadn't even thought about protection once she was in his arms.

His grim panic from the night before shot into her mind. The very fact that he hadn't even thought of birth control had shocked him beyond belief. She hadn't thought of it, either, but then again, she wasn't worried about a pregnancy. Had she subconsciously expected him to take care of it? Or had she simply not cared because she knew she wanted his child? Regardless of the reasons for her memory's short-circuits, she'd known the moment he'd said it that very little could make her happier than to bear Stone's baby.

She was married to the man she loved and she knew instinctively that a child would change their lives forever. Stone would never let his child grow up in a broken home. If she did become pregnant, they'd stay married.

And then she'd have much more than a year to show him that he loved her, too.

But she had no desire to trap him in any way. She'd never imagined a man could be so scared by a few little words, she thought tenderly. Though she hadn't expected him to respond in kind, it had still hurt a little that he had so easily dismissed her feelings. Obviously he had never considered love to be a part of their relationship. She could only be patient now, and hope that her confession would get him thinking about love, about her, about making their marriage a forever one.

A surge of love so strong it shook her moved through her. Slowly she reached back with her left hand and let it rest on his hip, gently running her thumb back and forth across his warm flesh, simply needing to touch him. After a moment, his even breathing changed. So did something else, she discovered with pleasure, wriggling her bottom back against him a little more.

"Good morning." His voice in her ear was deep and sleep-roughened. The hand at her hip slid up to cup her breast, plucking lightly at her nipple until it contracted into a small, hardened point that sent streamers of arousal down into her abdomen.

"Good morning," she returned. "Welcome home."

"I thought you already did that."

She giggled. Then all coherent thought fled as he leaned over her and caught her mouth in a deep, sweet kiss. When she had to breathe or die, he lay back again behind her. For an instant he rolled away, and she heard the sound of a foil packet tearing, then heard him quickly fitting himself with protection. He'd insisted on using protection the second time last night, too, though she'd told him he didn't have to. He'd gone still for a moment, then simply sighed, shaken his head and kissed her.

In a moment, he was back. His hand slid down over her body to her thighs and he urged her top leg up, draping it over his as he angled himself into the hot, tight crevice he'd made. She felt the column of blunt male flesh prodding at her and he lifted her leg a little higher, until suddenly, he flexed his hips and slid smoothly into her. She moaned, impaled on pleasure, and slipped her hand back to his taut, lean buttocks to pull him even closer, even deeper.

"Are you sore?" He stopped abruptly. "I didn't even think—"

"I'm fine," she said, shifting her hips and stroking the smooth, hot length of him, "now."

Stone nuzzled her hair aside and kissed the joining of her shoulder and her neck. He flattened his hand on her lower stomach, holding her steady as he moved against her. And again, she welcomed him home.

Afterward, he rolled to his back. She pulled the sheet over her, not comfortable enough with nudity yet to ignore her own modesty, watching as he disposed of their protection.

"I meant it, you know," she said quietly as his gaze met hers.

"Which 'it' are you referring to?" he asked cautiously.

"Everything," she said honestly. "I do love you. And if a baby is a result of this—" she indicated them "—I would be thrilled."

"What about school?" His voice was challenging. "Starting your own business? Or is that all just so much talk?"

"Of course not." She refused to let him pick a fight over this, though she suspected he would feel better if he were able to make her angry. "Having a family and a career don't have to be mutually exclusive." The moment the words left her mouth, she realized that to Stone, who had been the victim of a marriage in which that very thing had indeed been an issue, the two goals were in direct conflict with one another.

"Are you kidding?" He sat up abruptly and swung his feet over the side of the bed. "Women can comfort themselves with that 'I can do it all' mantra as much as they want. But the reality is that something suffers when they try to juggle too many balls." He slapped an angry hand down on the bed between them. "I have no intention of bringing children into this world to be tossed to whichever parent isn't as busy at the moment. In fact, I never plan to have children at all!"

Faith stared at him, shocked by the declaration. She understood that he felt he'd been the casualty of his mother's determination to have a career but she'd never imagined he would let it affect him to such an extent. If only she could get him to walk in his mother's shoes long enough to realize it hadn't been the simple, power-hungry decision he assumed it had been. Her heart ached for him as she understood exactly what his parents' differing points of view could cost him.

Could cost them both.

Slowly, seeing that insistence would only make him more intractable, she said, "I apologize for not understanding how you feel. We have plenty of time to think about children—" unless he threw her out when her year was up "—and I certainly would never try to talk you into doing something you don't want."

There was a long, tense silence.

Finally Stone heaved a huge sigh. He turned toward her, not away, and she knew an overwhelming relief as he took her in his arms. "I'm sorry, too," he said. "I shouldn't have gotten angry with you. We never talked about children because I didn't think it would ever be an issue. Hopefully it still won't be." He pressed a gentle kiss to her forehead. "Can we just enjoy this for now?"

"Of course," she murmured. She tilted her face up to his and kissed him sweetly, deeply, without reserve. With any luck at all, each day that passed would bring them a little closer, and he would see what a long life together could be like. And how very special it would be to add a child born of their love to their family.

After a final kiss, he rose from the bed and went into the bathroom. She rolled over to watch him walk away, admiring the way his wide shoulders tapered down to a lean waist, the way the muscles in his buttocks flexed as he walked, the strong, well-shaped columns of his legs. As he disappeared, her gaze fell on the clock beside the bed.

"Oh, no!" She suddenly realized it was Thursday, one of the days she'd set up to work for Smythe Corp. And she was going to be late if she didn't hurry. She bolted from the bed and headed for the door that connected their bedrooms.

Stone came out of the bathroom and followed her, unselfconsciously naked. She wrapped her robe around her then rushed to her dresser for fresh undergarments and panty hose, wishing she could be as blasé about her nudity.

"What's the rush?" He rested a shoulder against the doorway of her closet as she picked out a sedate gray-charcoal suit. "Do you have plans this morning?"

"I, um, yes." She skirted him and started for her bathroom, but he caught her by the waist and dragged her back against him.

"Can they wait?" He dropped his head and trailed a line of kisses down her neck, and she shivered as his hot breath blasted her sensitive nerve endings. "I thought we could take a bath together and then have breakfast."

She swallowed, tempted by his words, and her body heated at the image of the two of them in the big Jacuzzi tub in his bathroom. "I—can I take a rain check?" She cleared her throat. "I really do have some place I need to be. And don't you want to get back to your office?" Instinct warned her that explaining she was working for his mother probably wasn't the wisest course of action she could take.

"I've been in touch by phone, fax and e-mail," he said. "I hadn't planned on going in early today after traveling for all those hours. Where are you going?"

There was no help for it. She took a deep breath. "I have a temporary job."

His brows snapped together. After a moment, he said, "I thought you wanted to be able to spend time with your mother?"

"It's only a part-time thing," she said. "And it hasn't interfered with my time with Mama. She rests a lot."

"Where are you working? I'm surprised you were able to find anything suitable."

He meant that didn't expose her to the public, she knew. She took a deep breath. The thought of lying to him flitted across her mind and was rejected in the same instant. "Your mother offered me a position straightening out some records that were left in a mess by a departing employee."

"My *mother?*" His expression grew even more forbidding.

She swallowed. "The day we had lunch she asked me to consider it…"

"Why the hell didn't you say no?"

She squared her shoulders and lifted her chin. "Because I was bored. I wanted something to do, some kind of work and you wouldn't even consider it."

"You *have* things to do," he roared.

She'd never thought of herself as a temperamental person but the unfairness of his expectations refused to let her quail before his displeasure. "No," she said stonily. "I don't. The den is redecorated, the thank-yous are written and sent. I still have time to take on any other little projects you throw my way, but two days a week, I will be working at Smythe Corp."

Stone eyed her expression, apparently deciding he was going nowhere fast. "Fine," he said angrily. "Have a great time." He stalked back to his own room, closing the door between them with a definite snap and she winced, holding back tears.

She'd known he was going to be unhappy about her new job but she hadn't really thought he'd react quite so...strongly. Did it bother him because she would be in steady contact with his mother or because he simply didn't like not being able to control her every move?

Eight

He'd been an ass.

A horse's ass. A *big* horse's ass. Stone stared moodily out the window of his office at the gray Manhattan day. It was raining. He'd really been looking forward to some sunshine this morning, but when he'd stepped out the door to start the jogging that he tried to fit in four or five times a week, he'd been soaked to the skin in less than a minute. The only good thing about it was that Central Park had been nearly deserted, except for a few other hardy exercising idiots like himself.

God, what had he been thinking, to lay into Faith like that?

He hadn't been, he supposed. He was still jet-lagged from the unbearably long flights home. And he certainly hadn't gotten what he could call a full night's sleep last night.

He pinched the bridge of his nose between his thumb and forefinger. Last night.

The mere thought of it was enough to make him start to sweat. He'd woken with her in his arms and as his body had reacted to the sweet, soft lure of hers, he'd acknowledged what he'd been avoiding for days: he enjoyed having Faith in his life. He wanted to make this a real marriage, at least for the time they had left. He'd tried to stay away from her, but fate and Faith had tempted him until he couldn't resist anymore.

He couldn't quite remember why he'd thought it was such a bad idea. There was no reason they couldn't have a physical relationship while they were married. Unless, perhaps, he counted the fact that she might never speak to him again after the way he'd stormed off.

One thing that was certain—perhaps the only thing—was that he owed Faith an apology. He might not like her working for his mother, he might even— if he admitted the truth—feel betrayed in a small way, but he didn't own her. They had an agreement to which she was living up and anything she did that didn't jeopardize that was none of his business.

He didn't like the way that thought made him feel. *He wanted it to be his business, dammit!* He wanted her to be his wife in every way there was. He didn't just want her hostess skills or even her wonderfully responsive young body. He wanted her mind, her emotions, her commitment.

He shoved himself from his chair with an explosive curse. Oh, hell. Oh, no. Oh, hell, no. He was not going to fall into her trap.

Faith had made sure he knew how she felt—that

she wanted to make their marriage a reality in every way. And the knowing was powerfully seductive, the future calling to him with almost irresistible force. But long-term commitments were for other people. He wasn't dumb enough to believe he'd feel like this about Faith forever. Sure, he had friends who appeared to have happy marriages. But he also had friends whose marriages had wrecked them emotionally and financially, and even, in the case of one buddy whose wife had shot him for sleeping around on her, physically. His own parents, with all their money and resources, hadn't made it work.

He knew better than to believe in happy endings.

Still, she had said she loved him. And maybe she did. But his cynical side, the side that was doing its level best to preserve him from stupid, ill-conceived ideas born of passion, that side of him said, *Gee, the timing surely is convenient.*

Her mother was getting worse. He'd given Naomi Harrell a home, kept her companion, offered to provide her with more care. Faith cared deeply for her mother and would naturally appreciate his support. But would she tell him she loved him simply because of that?

She might if she were worried about what was going to happen once you cut her loose. She might if she wanted to ensure that you kept the funds flowing.

No way. His mind rejected the ugly notion. Faith had integrity and honor enough for two people. She'd been determined to secure care for her mother through other efforts before they'd married. She wouldn't stoop to the easy solution.

Would she?

Of course not. She was as aware of the terms of their marriage as he was. But damned if he was happy with them. When he tried to imagine what would happen next March, he failed utterly. He couldn't see himself without Faith. He couldn't see his home without her quiet influence or even, ridiculous as it seemed, her relatives. Before Faith had come, his elegant, upscale town house had been little more than an address to identify him. Sure, it had come to him from his father. But frankly, his memories of growing up in this house were less than stellar. It was a mausoleum. Or at least, it had been.

Now it was a home. When he came to breakfast, Clarice had brought the paper in for him already. Faith almost always saw him off, holding his coat and waving him out the door. When he came home in the evening, Faith and Naomi often were in the den, ensconced by the fireplace playing a board game. Sometimes Faith read to her mother, since Naomi's eyesight was deteriorating to the point that she was becoming unable to read. He had a wonderful new chair in the den, too, one that Faith had picked out herself.

And last night, he'd had just about the best night of his life.

So why was he still planning on getting rid of his wife at the end of a year?

He didn't know. And thinking about it was giving him a royal headache. What he really ought to be thinking about was how to get back in Faith's good graces. And if he were smart, he'd be thinking about what he could do to keep her so busy she wouldn't have time to go hunting for work, for his mother or anyone.

And then he had an idea.

* * *

She hadn't had the best day of her life. Though the assignment Eliza had given her was indeed a challenge, Faith's mind had drifted continually, rehashing the angry exchange with Stone that morning.

It just wasn't fair. Last night, he'd made her happier than she'd ever thought she could be. Then this morning, her happiness was ripped away with the angry words he'd thrown at her.

Faith sighed as she walked briskly from the subway station to the town house. Love was supposed to make people happy, not miserable.

When she came through the door, she was struck by the same feeling she always got when she entered her home…it was cozy, despite its size, and welcoming, despite her husband's anger. It had truly become home. Leaving it was going to be one of the hardest things she'd—

An odd scrabbling sound behind her startled her as she hung her coat over a hook on the coat rack. She whirled. A small furry creature was barreling toward her, skidding and slipping on the smooth polished hardwood floor.

A puppy!

"It's for you," said a deep male voice, and she looked up to see Stone lounging against the door frame at the end of the hall.

She dropped to her knees and gathered up the puppy, talking nonsense to the wriggly little black-and-tan bundle, giving herself time to collect her thoughts. He didn't sound angry anymore. Cautiously she said, "What kind is it?" as she held the puppy up to her cheek. She laughed as the little tongue lapped at her cheek.

"She's a German Shepherd," he said. "Do you like her?"

"She's adorable! She's so tiny."

"She won't be that size for long. I thought she would be a good companion when you're walking around the park alone." He walked forward as she got to her feet with the puppy in her arms and to her shock and pleasure, he drew her close. "I'm sorry about this morning." He dropped his head and sought her mouth before she could speak, masterfully teasing her into a response that flared wildly between them. Then he tore his mouth away from hers. "Will you forgive me? It's none of my business what you do with your time."

She was stunned. What had produced this sea change? "Of course," she said, resting her head against his shoulder. "I'm sorry I didn't tell you before."

"Well," he said in a teasing tone, "I seem to recall that we were somewhat preoccupied...before." Then he set her away from him. "What should we name her?" he asked, nodding at the puppy.

"I don't know! Have Mama and Clarice seen her yet?"

He laughed. "Yes. They were bitten by the love bug at first sight. Or should I say first lick?"

She giggled. Then she snapped her fingers. "That's perfect. How about Lovebug?"

"Lovebug?" He looked dubious. "You'd really make me stand on the streets of New York with a German Shepherd named Lovebug?"

When he put it that way…"Oh, well," she said. "Back to the drawing board."

"It's got a certain cachet, though," he said. "Lovebug." He bent his knees so that he was eye level with the dog in her arms. "Are you a lovebug?"

She smiled at him. "You sound just like a doting daddy."

"That's what I was afraid of."

There was an instant of awkward silence as they both remembered the night before.

"We'd better take her out," he said at the same time that she said, "What will we do with her at night?"

They both laughed, and the moment passed. He put a hand at her back and guided her to the back of the house, where they took Lovebug outside. Then he showed her a crate in the kitchen. "The breeder told me it would be a good idea to get her used to being crated," he said. "For trips to the vet, or if we're away, or if we have parties and we want to protect or confine her. Apparently a lot of dogs like them so much they voluntarily sleep in them if the door is left open." He pointed to the table, where several books and a variety of leashes and toys lay. "I got a few things the breeder recommended."

She shook her head, amused. "You don't do anything halfway, do you?"

"Why don't you let me show you?" His voice dropped intimately.

A thrill of arousal shot through her. "What will we do with Lovebug?"

"Try out the crate?" he suggested. So they did, and to her amazement, the puppy sniffed around her new domain, wrestled once or twice with a large stuffed parrot, and then circled three times and fell asleep on the fleecy dog bed Stone had purchased.

"Hot damn!" he said. "Shall we try out the tub?" He took her hand and pulled her up the stairs into his room.

"We haven't even eaten dinner yet," she protested.

"Later." His voice was a rough growl. He tugged her into his arms and wrapped them around her tightly, so that every inch of her was locked against every inch of him. "I want you," he said. "I didn't get a damn thing done today because all I could think about was you."

She was stunned. And so happy she thought she might just burst. He'd brought her a puppy. A puppy that wasn't going to be anywhere near full-grown in less than a year, meaning...? She couldn't even let herself hope.

But now, now he was telling her things that she'd longed to hear, that she'd never imagined she would. He wanted her. He'd thought of her all day. "I thought of you, too," she said. "I—" But she didn't get a chance to tell him she loved him.

His mouth closed over hers as he bent and lifted her into his arms. He carried her up the steps and into the bathroom, where she discovered that he hadn't been kidding about trying out the tub.

Later, they ordered a pizza and ate it in front of the fire. Stone propped his back against the couch afterward and pulled her against his side, stretching his long legs out and sighing. "I'm still acclimating to the time change. I'm beat."

"Was your trip fruitful?" she asked, curling against him and laying her head on his shoulder. She kept her voice light, trying for an easy conversational tone as she stroked the puppy that lay in his lap.

He rolled his head, stretching the taut muscles in his neck. "Yes. We're going to begin the application process to open a plant in Beijing. With a little luck and a lot of greasing of official palms, we might be up and running in twelve more months or so."

He was talking about his work! She hid her elation and said, "Isn't there an awful lot of corruption in China? How are you going to control your costs?"

"I've factored in a certain amount of overhead simply because of that. And I'm using American managers, at least for the setup, until we get a true cost picture. Once things stabilize, we might hire local managers."

"But by then you'll know the costs and if things changed drastically you'd know something funny was going on."

"Exactly." He hesitated. "I'm going to have to go away again next week."

"Oh." She let her disappointment show in her tone. "Where to this time?"

"Dallas."

"I'll miss you."

"And I'll miss you." He turned his head and kissed her temple, and her heart doubled its beat. Stone wasn't just acting like a man who had the hots for a woman. He was acting as if he really cared for her. Then he spoke again. "I thought about asking you to go along, but I'll be so busy you probably would see very little of me. I've managed to schedule five days of work into three, though, so it won't be a long trip."

"Good." She traced a pattern in the thick mat of

hair that covered his chest, exposed by the shirt he'd thrown on and hadn't bothered to button. "I can see I'm going to develop an aversion to your absences."

"Then I'll just have to devote extra time to you while I'm here." He lifted the puppy and surged to his feet, starting for the kitchen. "Let's put her in her crate and go to bed."

"That would be nice," she said demurely.

He looked back as he straightened from the crate, catching the gleam in her eye, and laughed as he started toward her. "It'll be a whole lot more than 'nice,' and you know it."

The following week raced by at the speed of light. He made love to Faith every chance he got, and if she could be more radiant, he couldn't imagine how. She lit up whenever he came into the room, her pleasure in his presence clearly apparent. Stone decided that if all marriages were like his, no one would ever get divorced.

The thought sobered him slightly. When they'd married, he'd planned a quiet annulment at the end of twelve months. Now there was no chance of that. He and Faith would have to divorce. The very word left a bad taste in his mouth.

He was scheduled to leave for Dallas on an afternoon flight. That morning, he went in to the office for a few hours, then came home to pack. Faith sat on the bed and watched as he efficiently gathered his clothing and folded it into the suit bag he was taking.

"You're awfully good at that," she said. "I guess you get a lot of practice."

"Practice makes perfect," he parroted. He looked at her, seated cross-legged on his bed—and suddenly, he knew he was going to have to have her one more time before he left. Her lovely face was woebegone at the prospect of separation; he knew just how she felt. The thought of sleeping without her was making him more than a little desperate.

Setting aside the briefs he was stuffing into corners, he stepped toward her, his hands going to his belt, swiftly opening his pants.

"Stone!" she said. "You've already had your send-off."

"Ah, but that was goodbye." He put his hands on her thighs and slid them up beneath the skirt she wore, dragging down her pantyhose and the thong he'd watched her shimmy into that morning, throwing them across the room. "This," he said, positioning himself and bracing his body over hers as he slowly pushed into the hot, welcoming depths of her body, "is my incentive to hurry home."

Her eyes were dazed, her expression so sensually intent that it set fire to his already raging need for her. He lifted her thighs and draped them over his shoulders, beginning a quick, hard rhythm. She bit down on her lip and moaned, then her eyes flared wide and she arched up to meet him. It was a fast, frantic coupling. He was driven by a need he didn't fully understand, some primitive urge to stamp her as his, and he hammered himself into her receptive body until she convulsed in his arms. Immediately he followed her, feeling himself spilling forcefully into her until he lay over her, panting.

Faith lifted her arms, which had fallen limp to her sides, and clasped his head in her palms. She gave him her mouth in a sweet, deep kiss that he returned in full measure. When she tore her lips from his, she gasped, "I hate it when you're gone."

"I know, baby." He grinned at the pouty expression on her face, kissing her again. Faith wasn't generally moody; she must really be minding this. "I'm sorry. I'll try to cut down on my traveling from now on."

"I'd like that," she said. "I had visions of spending the next couple of decades watching you pack a couple of times a month."

"Faith—" Her words were entirely too seductive, slipping into his mind and twining around the need for her that he couldn't admit, even to himself. With an effort, he recalled his original proposition. One year. That was all he'd ever promised her.

"I love you," she said. He closed his eyes against the stark emotion pooling in hers, defensive anger rippling through him. Hadn't she understood anything he'd said that first night they'd made love? But she continued. "I know you think you don't want children now, but you might change your mind one of these days, and I'd hate for our child to grow up wondering where Daddy is half the time. As it is, Lovebug is going to be devastated. She worships you. I thought in a couple of years maybe we could get her a companion—"

"Faith!"

She finally stopped, and her shock at his tone was evident.

Fighting himself as well as her, he said, "I told you before that I don't want children. And does the phrase 'temporary marriage' ring any bells with you?" The words were harsh with frustration.

Immediately he regretted the question. She recoiled from the words as if he'd struck her. Slowly, she said, "We've been talking—sharing—everything, which I assumed meant we were growing closer. You got the dog, which I assumed meant we'd be sharing her in our future. You've made love to me every chance we got, which I assumed meant more than simply sex. Did I assume wrong?"

He was sweating. Pure fear took over. What if he let himself believe her? He wasn't sure he'd survive if she left him one day. "You knew from the very beginning that this arrangement had a definite end in sight." Forget the fact that he'd been wondering if there was any need to end it. Ever.

Her whole body stiffened. She immediately pushed at his shoulders, trying to free herself. He held her down with implacable force, their bodies still joined, but she turned her head to the side, shutting him out. Tears trickled from beneath her eyelids and ran across the bridge of her nose to disappear into the hair at her temple. He swore, dragging himself back away from her and shoving his clothing roughly into place.

Faith scrambled backward away from him, off the far side of the bed, where she bent her head and ignored him while she pulled her skirt into place, ignoring the fact that she was wearing nothing beneath it. Finally she took an audible breath and raised her head. Her gaze was so tortured and filled with pain that it struck him like a blow.

"I asked you a question earlier. You haven't answered it." Her voice was steady but her eyes were swimming with tears. "I assumed our lovemaking was more than sex. Was I wrong?"

No! Admitting anything would make him vulnerable. He hesitated.

And in that fatal second, he saw that whatever he said wasn't going to be enough.

"Never mind," she said. She turned toward the door.

"I told you before that it was easy to confuse love and lust," he threw at her back, furious at her for forcing this confrontation. "You're too young to know the difference."

She stopped. Turned. And shot him a look of such fury that he was shocked. Then the fury drained away, right before his eyes, leaving her face a stark study in anguish. "You're wrong," she said, her voice breaking. "But if all this is to you is a case of lust, don't expect sex when you come home again. Because I'll be looking for someone to *love*."

"Wait," he said, but she was already gone, the slam of the door echoing around his bedroom. He sank onto the bed, putting his head in his hands. What in hell had just happened? Guilt tore through him. He'd broken her heart. Deliberately. Using words like weapons to hurt her.

And he was afraid she was never going to forgive him.

Why? *Why* had he done that? He could have made his point in a gentler way. But she'd rattled him so badly that he hadn't been able to think for the panic clouding his brain.

He rose, intending to find her and demand that they talk this out, to apologize and grovel if it would keep her from looking at him as if he were lower than an earthworm. She would forgive him. She'd been the epitome of patience and understanding since they'd married; it was only to be expected that she would get frustrated and lose it occasionally. But she'd forgiven him before, each time he'd hurt her by reminding her that the marriage was temporary, that her feelings were transient. Once she calmed down, she'd forgive him again. *She had to.*

Why? asked the smug little voice in his head. *You didn't want her emotions.*

But he did. He took a breath so deep that his shirt seams strained. Oh, God, he did. He wanted her love, her understanding, her happiness, every emotion she felt.

Then the unmistakable sound of the back door closing caught his attention. He rushed to the window in time to see her slide into the smaller of his two cars and disappear down the street.

He was astounded. His gaze shot to the intimate apparel she'd left discarded on the floor. Unless she had underwear stashed in her purse or something, Faith had just left without even bothering to get fresh underwear.

Knowing her as he did, that realization alarmed him more than anything. Faith was the most ladylike of ladies outside their bedroom door. She would never do something so risqué without extreme provocation.

And that seemingly small action told him far more effectively than any words that *she considered their marriage to be over.*

The panic he'd been trying to subdue punched him full in the chest. Too late, he saw what had been within his reach all this time: a long happy life with the woman he loved at his side. But he'd driven her away with his selfish, self-protective actions...

And now he had nothing.

* * *

He canceled the Dallas trip, clinging to a dwindling hope that she would come home and forgive him.

But Faith never came home that night. He called her former roommates, the only friends he knew she had, but they professed not to have seen her.

He went to work the next day because the alternative was answering unanswerable questions from Clarice and Naomi. He had a lot of time to think while he sat in his office trying unsuccessfully to work. He'd tried to call Faith at home several times, but every time the machine had picked up. He'd known, in his heart, that she wouldn't answer even if she were there, but he'd had to try.

More than once, he picked up the phone to call a private investigator to track her down. But each time, he'd set the phone back in its cradle unused. Lunch was as unappealing as breakfast had been and he barely touched his meal.

That night, he explained to Naomi and Clarice that he and Faith had had a misunderstanding and that she'd gone away for a few days. Her mother was clearly alarmed, saying over and over again that Faith would never just go off without telling her. Stone spent an hour reassuring her, telling her that he was the messenger Faith had chosen, that she would be back.

And he'd see that she did return. Even if it meant him moving out.

Five days passed, with the weekend sandwiched in between. On the morning of the fifth day, Faith finally acknowledged that Stone wasn't coming after her. She knew what kind of determination and drive he had. If he'd wanted to find her, he'd have made it happen within hours of her leaving.

He didn't want her.

She lay in the spare bedroom of the apartment that Eliza Smythe's receptionist had offered to share with her when she'd learned of Faith's dilemma and sobbed silently into her pillow. She should be dealing with this better. Hadn't she already cried enough to fill a bathtub?

It was time to contact him, she decided. To let him know she would return and honor her commitment. The very thought brought fresh tears. But she'd made a promise and she intended to keep it. The only change would be that she planned to move into the set of rooms her mother and Clarice shared. That way, she could avoid Stone altogether, except for times when they had to appear publicly.

She couldn't imagine how she was going to get through the rest of the year.

Still, people didn't die from broken hearts. She'd be starting school in another month, and since she had nothing else to think of, she could double the class load she'd intended to take. That would keep her from simply giving up. She hoped.

She couldn't give up! She had responsibilities that were bigger than her own problems. Once she had her degree and a full-time job she could cover the cost of her mother's care herself. And maybe if she worked hard enough and long enough, she'd be able to forget the man she loved.

The man who didn't love her.

* * *

He headed for his mother's office, praying that Faith still was coming to work there twice a week. The shock on the face of the young receptionist at the front desk would have amused him at any other time. Today, all his concentration was focused on meeting with his mother.

He was directed to Eliza Smythe's office, but as he strode down the hallway on the third floor, his mother came to meet him. "Stone! Welcome to Smythe Corp."

"Thank you." He realized abruptly how small she was. She had looked tiny and defenseless as she came toward him.

"I presume this isn't a social call," Eliza said briskly. "Come into my office and we'll talk."

Defenseless. Hah.

He followed her through a quietly elegant outer office to her own, a feminine mirror-image of his, with all the necessary bells and whistles softened by quiet colors and soft fabrics.

"Have a seat," his mother invited. She seated herself in one of the wing chairs flanking a small glass table rather than behind her desk.

He took the other seat and inhaled deeply. He'd spent his life rejecting his mother. It wasn't easy to ask for her help. "Faith has left me," he said abruptly.

Eliza's expression became guarded. "I'm sorry to hear that. I like your wife."

"So do I. I want her back."

His mother studied him for long enough to make him repress the urge to squirm in his seat like a schoolboy. "We don't always get what we want. Why do you want her back?"

"Because." He floundered, unable to force himself to say the words that would leave him vulnerable. "She's my wife."

"Well, that's sure to sway her," Eliza said. She leaned forward. "Why did she leave?"

"We had a...disagreement," he said. "I came here to find out if she's still working for you. I need your help to get her to talk to me."

"Why should I help you?"

"You're my mother!"

"Interesting that you should remember that now." She was unmerciful. "Look, Stone, I made no secret of the fact that I thought your marriage was just a ruse to get your hands on Smythe Corp. But once I saw you two together...I was pleased. And as I've gotten to know Faith better, I think she's perfect for you."

"She *is* perfect," he said. "I just didn't figure that out until too late."

"You wouldn't just be trying to convince me of this because of our agreement regarding your inheritance?"

"There's nothing I want less at the moment than this company." And he meant it. "If it would bring Faith back, you could give it to the first stranger on the street."

His mother's eyebrows rose. "You're serious," she said, and there was pleased wonder in her tone.

"Very." He sighed. "You weren't wrong. Faith and I had a bargain. I married her to satisfy your conditions. She married me because in return I agreed to take care of her mother."

"Which you were doing, anyway."

He was startled. "Says who?"

"I did a little checking into your life before I made my offer," she said coolly. "Imagine my surprise when I found out you were supporting the Harrell ladies lock, stock and barrel."

"Faith was equally surprised," he confessed. "She just found out a few months ago."

"Ah. She confronted you, did she?"

Was his mother a mind reader? "All that's history now," he said. "I just want her back."

"Maybe she doesn't want to come back. What did you do to make her leave?" Eliza hadn't gotten to be a success by dancing around the issues.

"I, um, let her think I didn't love her," he said. It was hard to admit it, much less say it aloud.

"I see." She steepled her fingers. "And you want me to do what? Convince her that you do? Tell you when she's working?"

"All I want," he said, desperate and not caring anymore if he sounded it, "is a chance to talk to her. Then, if she still wants to leave, she can."

"You would lose Smythe Corp." Eliza reminded him, probing the depth of his sincerity.

"I don't give a damn!" he shouted, finally losing patience with explanations. "Hell, I'd even sell Lachlan if it would bring Faith back."

There was a moment of profound silence in the room. He glared defiantly at his mother. Eliza rose and walked around her desk. His heart sank. She wasn't going to help him. It was poetic justice for all the times when she'd tried to be a part of his life and he'd shut her out.

Well, he'd sit in the street and wait for Faith to come out if that was what it took to track her down.

Eliza hit a button on her speakerphone. "Hallie, would you send Faith in here, please?"

"Yes, ma'am."

A moment later, the door opened and Faith started through. His gaze was riveted to her. In the part of him that wasn't absorbed in steeping himself in his wife's presence, he was astonished. His mother must have sent for her when he'd arrived!

But then Faith saw him. She stopped in her tracks and her face was weary and wan, her eyelids puffy. She looked ill. After one quick glance, she ignored him and spoke to Eliza. "You sent for me?"

"There's a visitor to see you," Eliza said.

"There's no one that I want to see." Her voice shook and she bent her head, studying the carpet. He restrained himself from going to her and forcing her to acknowledge his presence, to grab her and hold her so she could never get away from him again. It was obvious that Faith was going to turn right around and walk out the door if he didn't let his mother handle this. The irony didn't escape him. How could it be that his mother, who had been absent for so many years when he'd have given anything for her attention, was the only person who could make his world right now?

"Faith." The president and CEO of Smythe Corp. waited until Faith looked up again. "My son is a very smart man in many ways. But in others, he's…a little dim." She smiled fondly at him. "And since I contributed to his desire to protect himself and avoid commitment, I feel bound to try to repair the damage. Will you listen to him?"

"That's all I want," Stone said quickly. "Just listen. And then, if you still want to leave, I won't stop you.''

She had swung her gaze to him when he began to speak, and he saw doubt, sorrow, hope, and myriad other emotions tumbling in her eyes before she made her face blank again. She shrugged. ''All right,'' she said in a barely audible voice.

Nine

"**W**hy didn't you just hire someone to find me?" she asked. She looked at the floor because she was afraid if she looked at him, the love she couldn't banish would be written all over her face. She didn't have any intention of letting him trample her heart more than he already had.

He shook his head. "It was my mistake. It was mine to fix."

"You could have sent me flowers, or jewels, to ask me to come home."

"Baby, I'll shower you with both if that's what you want," he said huskily. "But those are things. Anyone could send gifts. I didn't think that was the way to your heart."

"I didn't think my heart had anything to do with our marriage." She couldn't hide the note of anguish and her voice wobbled as she fought back tears.

He winced. "I didn't, either, in the beginning," he said quietly. "But I've found that your heart is essential, not just to our marriage but to my survival." He started across the room toward her. "And I've also found that I have to give you mine in return, because it's withering away without you."

She lifted her head and stared at him, rejecting the words. The moment she moved, he stopped immediately, as if he were afraid of startling her into flight. "You don't have to tell me that," she said wearily. "I'd already decided I have to come back and stay for the rest of the year."

"How can I convince you that I love you?" he asked her. "How can I convince you that I need you to love me?"

"You don't have to say that!" she cried. "I just told you I'll keep my end of our bargain."

"There is no bargain," he told her, his gaze steady and warm with an emotion she couldn't let herself believe in. "I told my mother she could give her company to someone else. I don't want it if it means I can't have you."

Her heart skipped a beat, then settled into a mad rhythm that threatened to burst out of her chest. "You can't do that. This company has always been in your family." *And part of your dream is to put your family back together.*

"Watch me." He rose and walked to the door, opening it. "Mother, would you please come in here?"

Eliza appeared in the doorway, her gaze questioning first one of them and then the other. "Yes?"

"What did I tell you before you brought Faith in here?"

His mother looked perplexed. "You mean about loving her or about giving up the company?" She turned to Faith. "Actually I believe his words were, 'I'd even sell Lachlan if it would bring Faith back.'"

Faith's face drained of color. Stone leaped forward, afraid she was going to faint as she groped for a chair. His mother went out again, closing the door behind her but he barely noticed. He gathered his wife into his arms, turning to sit in the wing chair and pulling her into his lap.

She didn't even struggle, just lay passively with her face buried in his shoulder.

She was warm, smelling of the indefinable essence of her, a scent he would recognize anywhere, and he nuzzled his nose into her hair. "God, I've missed you." His voice shook, surprising him as he savored the weight of her body pressed against him. She still didn't move, didn't respond, and he started to worry. "Faith?"

Slowly, she pushed away from him and sat up. "You think I'm too young to know the difference between love and sex."

"No." He shook his head slowly, holding her gaze, trying to communicate the depth of his feeling to her. "The truth is, I was *afraid* you were too young. I felt like I was taking advantage of you— you hadn't known enough men to know whether you loved me or not. And whether or not I wanted to admit it, I was falling for you. I was afraid. Afraid you'd grow up and fall out of love with me, afraid to believe in forever." He ran his palms slowly up and down her arms. "Now," he said, "now I don't give one flying damn if you're too young or not, because *I* know the difference." He swallowed, his throat closing up. "And what we have is love."

He saw her face change, just a slight relaxation of the tense muscles. She believed him! "I love you," he said again. "Forever."

"Forever." Her voice wobbled. "I love you, too."

He sought her mouth, relief almost a painful sensation as she kissed him back. God, he'd been afraid he'd never know her kiss again. He lifted his head a fraction. "As long as we live."

She gazed earnestly into his eyes. "It's all right if you don't want children. We'll have each other."

He considered her offer. "Thank you, but I've changed my mind about so many things I think I'll change it about that, too." He took her face in his hands. "I want to give you babies. I want to be there when they're born, and every day of our lives after that. I want to see your mother's face the first time we put her grandchild in her arms."

"And your mother's." Tears glimmered in her eyes but she was smiling.

"And my mother's," he repeated. He glanced around the room. "I guess she's going to be smug about this for the rest of my life." But his tone was fond. Somewhere inside him, he'd discovered that he could accept his past. He knew he and his mother would have to talk, because she felt obliged to explain. But he also knew it wasn't going to matter. She would be a part of his future.

Faith laughed. "How did she know to call for me?"

"If I had to guess, I'd say that little receptionist out front probably gave her the headsup. She looked like she'd seen a ghost when I walked in."

"'That little receptionist' happens to have become a friend of mine," Faith told him. "I've been staying with her."

Another mystery solved. "I guess I have to thank her, then, for taking care of you."

"We might have to buy her new pillows," she said. "I've sobbed into all of hers so much they're permanently soaked."

He stroked her cheek, sobered by her words. "No more sobbing. Promise?"

She smiled tenderly, her hand coming up to stroke the back of his neck. "Promise."

He kissed her again, pulling her close and the caress quickly turned to a searing passion as he stroked her body, unable to get enough of her after the days of worry. "I want you," he said in a low voice. "I want to get started on making a baby right away."

"Not here!" She straightened immediately, looking shocked.

"It is going to be my office some day," he reminded her, loving the prim and proper streak that was as much a part of her as her love for him.

"Well, it isn't yet!"

He laughed, intoxicated by the feel of her in his arms again. "Then let's go home, wife, so I can show you how much I love you and need you."

*   *   *   *   *

Look for Anne Marie Winston's
next Silhouette Desire,
BILLIONAIRE BACHELORS: GARRETT,
in May 2002.

April 2002
MR. TEMPTATION
#1430 by Cait London

HEARTBREAKERS

Don't miss the first book in
Cait London's sensual new
miniseries featuring to-die-for
heroes and the women they love.

May 2002
HIS MAJESTY, M.D.
#1435 by Leanne Banks

Leanne Banks continues
her exciting miniseries about
a royal family faced with the
ultimate temptation—love.

June 2002
A COWBOY'S PURSUIT
#1441 by Anne McAllister

Bestselling author
Anne McAllister's
sexy cowboy heroes
are determined to win
the hearts of the women
they've chosen.

MAN OF THE MONTH

Some men are made for lovin'—and you're sure to love
these three upcoming men of the month!

Available at your favorite retail outlet.

Silhouette®
Where love comes alive™

This Mother's Day Give Your Mom A Royal Treat

Win a fabulous one-week vacation in Puerto Rico for you and your mother at the luxurious Inter-Continental San Juan Resort & Casino. The prize includes round trip airfare for two, breakfast daily and a mother and daughter day of beauty at the beachfront hotel's spa.

INTER·CONTINENTAL
San Juan
RESORT & CASINO

Here's all you have to do:

Tell us in 100 words or less how your mother helped with the romance in your life. It may be a story about your engagement, wedding or those boyfriends when you were a teenager or any other romantic advice from your mother. The entry will be judged based on its originality, emotionally compelling nature and sincerity. See official rules on following page.

Send your entry to:

Mother's Day Contest

In Canada	**In U.S.A.**
P.O. Box 637	P.O. Box 9076
Fort Erie, Ontario	3010 Walden Ave.
L2A 5X3	Buffalo, NY
	14269-9076

Or enter online at www.eHarlequin.com

HARLEQUIN MOTHER'S DAY CONTEST 2216
OFFICIAL RULES
NO PURCHASE NECESSARY TO ENTER

Two ways to enter:

• **Via The Internet:** Log on to the Harlequin romance website (www.eHarlequin.com) anytime beginning 12:01 a.m. E.S.T., January 1, 2002 through 11:59 p.m. E.S.T., April 1, 2002 and follow the directions displayed on-line to enter your name, address (including zip code), e-mail address and in 100 words or fewer, describe how your mother helped with the romance in your life.

• **Via Mail:** Handprint (or type) on an 8 1/2" x 11" plain piece of paper, your name, address (including zip code) and e-mail address (if you have one), and in 100 words or fewer, describe how your mother helped with the romance in your life. Mail your entry via first-class mail to: Harlequin Mother's Day Contest 2216, (in the U.S.) P.O. Box 9076, Buffalo, NY 14269-9076; (in Canada) P.O. Box 637, Fort Erie, Ontario, Canada L2A 5X3.

For eligibility, entries must be submitted either through a completed Internet transmission or postmarked no later than 11:59 p.m. E.S.T., April 1, 2002 (mail-in entries must be received by April 9, 2002). Limit one entry per person, household address and e-mail address. On-line and/or mailed entries received from persons residing in geographic areas in which entry is not permissible will be disqualified.

Entries will be judged by a panel of judges, consisting of members of the Harlequin editorial, marketing and public relations staff using the following criteria:
  • Originality - 50%
  • Emotional Appeal - 25%
  • Sincerity - 25%

In the event of a tie, duplicate prizes will be awarded. Decisions of the judges are final.

Prize: A 6-night/7-day stay for two at the Inter-Continental San Juan Resort & Casino, including round-trip coach air transportation from gateway airport nearest winner's home (approximate retail value: $4,000). Prize includes breakfast daily and a mother and daughter day of beauty at the beachfront hotel's spa. Prize consists of only those items listed as part of the prize. Prize is valued in U.S. currency.

All entries become the property of Torstar Corp. and will not be returned. No responsibility is assumed for lost, late, illegible, incomplete, inaccurate, non-delivered or misdirected mail or misdirected e-mail, for technical, hardware or software failures of any kind, lost or unavailable network connections, or failed, incomplete, garbled or delayed computer transmission or any human error which may occur in the receipt or processing of the entries in this Contest.

Contest open only to residents of the U.S. (except Colorado) and Canada, who are 18 years of age or older and is void wherever prohibited by law; all applicable laws and regulations apply. Any litigation within the Province of Quebec respecting the conduct or organization of a publicity contest may be submitted to the Régie des alcools, des courses et des jeux for a ruling. Any litigation respecting the awarding of a prize may be submitted to the Régie des alcools, des courses et des jeux only for the purpose of helping the parties reach a settlement. Employees and immediate family members of Torstar Corp. and D.L. Blair, Inc., their affiliates, subsidiaries and all other agencies, entities and persons connected with the use, marketing or conduct of this Contest are not eligible to enter. Taxes on prize are the sole responsibility of winner. Acceptance of any prize offered constitutes permission to use winner's name, photograph or other likeness for the purposes of advertising, trade and promotion on behalf of Torstar Corp., its affiliates and subsidiaries without further compensation to the winner, unless prohibited by law.

Winner will be determined no later than April 15, 2002 and be notified by mail. Winner will be required to sign and return an Affidavit of Eligibility form within 15 days after winner notification. Non-compliance within that time period may result in disqualification and an alternate winner may be selected. Winner of trip must execute a Release of Liability prior to ticketing and must possess required travel documents (e.g. Passport, photo ID) where applicable. Travel must be completed within 12 months of selection and is subject to traveling companion completing and returning a Release of Liability prior to travel; and hotel and flight accommodations availability. Certain restrictions and blackout dates may apply. No substitution of prize permitted by winner. Torstar Corp. and D.L. Blair, Inc., their parents, affiliates, and subsidiaries are not responsible for errors in printing or electronic presentation of Contest, or entries. In the event of printing or other errors which may result in unintended prize values or duplication of prizes, all affected entries shall be null and void. If for any reason the Internet portion of the Contest is not capable of running as planned, including infection by computer virus, bugs, tampering, unauthorized intervention, fraud, technical failures, or any other causes beyond the control of Torstar Corp. which corrupt or affect the administration, secrecy, fairness, integrity or proper conduct of the Contest, Torstar Corp. reserves the right, at its sole discretion, to disqualify any individual who tampers with the entry process and to cancel, terminate, modify or suspend the Contest or the Internet portion thereof. In the event the Internet portion must be terminated a notice will be posted on the website and all entries received prior to termination will be judged in accordance with these rules. In the event of a dispute regarding an on-line entry, the entry will be deemed submitted by the authorized holder of the e-mail account submitted at the time of entry. Authorized account holder is defined as the natural person who is assigned to an e-mail address by an Internet access provider, on-line service provider or other organization that is responsible for arranging e-mail address for the domain associated with the submitted e-mail address. Torstar Corp. and/or D.L. Blair Inc. assumes no responsibility for any computer injury or damage related to or resulting from accessing and/or downloading any sweepstakes material. Rules are subject to any requirements/limitations imposed by the FCC. **Purchase or acceptance of a product offer does not improve your chances of winning.**

For winner's name (available after May 1, 2002), send a self-addressed, stamped envelope to: Harlequin Mother's Day Contest Winners 2216, P.O. Box 4200 Blair, NE 68009-4200 or you may access the www.eHarlequin.com Web site through June 3, 2002.

Contest sponsored by Torstar Corp., P.O. Box 9042, Buffalo, NY 14269-9042.

presents

DYNASTIES: THE **CONNELLYS**

A brand-new miniseries about the Connellys of Chicago,
a wealthy, powerful American family tied by blood to the
royal family of the island kingdom of Altaria.
They're wealthy, powerful and rocked by
scandal, betrayal...and passion!

Look for a whole year of glamorous and
utterly romantic tales in 2002:

January: **TALL, DARK & ROYAL by Leanne Banks**

February: **MATERNALLY YOURS by Kathie DeNosky**

March: **THE SHEIKH TAKES A BRIDE by Caroline Cross**

April: **THE SEAL'S SURRENDER by Maureen Child**

May: **PLAIN JANE & DOCTOR DAD by Kate Little**

June: **AND THE WINNER GETS...MARRIED! by Metsy Hingle**

July: **THE ROYAL & THE RUNAWAY BRIDE by Kathryn Jensen**

August: **HIS E-MAIL ORDER WIFE by Kristi Gold**

September: **THE SECRET BABY BOND by Cindy Gerard**

October: **CINDERELLA'S CONVENIENT HUSBAND**
by Katherine Garbera

November: **EXPECTING...AND IN DANGER by Eileen Wilks**

December: **CHEROKEE MARRIAGE DARE**
by Sheri WhiteFeather

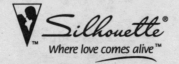

Where love comes alive™